after dark,
my sweet

after dark, my sweet

my sweet

jim thompson

 BLACK LIZARD / VINTAGE CRIME

vintage books • a division of random house, inc. • new york

First Black Lizard/Vintage Crime Edition, October 1990

ISBN 0-679-73247-0
Library of Congress Catalog Card Number: 90-50250

Manufactured in the United States of America
10   9   8   7   6   5   4   3   2   1

after dark,
my sweet

I rode a streetcar to the edge of the city limits, then I started to walk, swinging the old thumb whenever I saw a car coming. I was dressed pretty good—white shirt, brown slacks and sport shoes. I'd had a shower at the railroad station and a hair-trim in a barber college, so all in all I looked okay. But no one would stop for me. There'd been a lot of hitchhike robberies in that section, and people just weren't taking chances.

Around four in the afternoon, after I'd walked about ten miles, I came to this roadhouse. I went on past it a little ways, walking slower and slower, arguing with myself. I lost the argument—the part of me that was on-the-beam lost it—and I went back.

The bartender slopped a beer down in front of me. He scooped up the change I'd laid on the counter, sat down on his stool again, and picked up a newspaper. I said something about it was sure a hot day. He grunted without looking up. I said it was a nice pleasant little place he had there and that he certainly knew how to keep his beer cold. He grunted again.

I looked down at my beer, feeling the short hairs rising on the back of my neck. I guessed—I knew—that I should never have come in here. I should never go in any place where people might not be nice and polite to me. That's all they have to do, you know. Just be as nice to me as I am to them. I've been in four institutions, and my classification card always reads just about the same:

> *William ("Kid") Collins:* Blond, extremely handsome; very strong, agile. Mild criminal tendencies or none, according to environmental factors. Mild multiple neuroses (environmental) Psychosis, Korsakoff (no syndrome) induced by shock; aggravated by

worry. Treatment: absolute rest, quiet, whole-
some food and surroundings. Collins is amiable, polite,
patient, but may be very dangerous if aroused . . .

I finished the beer, and ordered another one. I sauntered
back to the restroom and washed my face in cold water. I
wondered, staring at myself in the mirror, where I'd be this
time tomorrow and why I was bothering to go anywhere
since every place was just like the last one. I wondered why
I hadn't stayed where I was—a week ago and a thousand
miles from here—and whether it wouldn't be smart to go
back. Of course, they hadn't been doing me much good
there. They were too overcrowded, too under-staffed, too
hard up for money. But they'd been pretty nice to me, and
if I hadn't gotten so damned restless, and if they hadn't
made it so easy to escape . . . It was so easy, you know,
you'd almost think they wanted you to do it.

I'd just walked off across the fields and into the forest. And
when I came out to the highway on the other side, there was a
guy fixing a tire on his car. He didn't see me. He never knew
what hit him. I dragged him back into the trees, took the sev-
enty bucks he was carrying and tramped on into town. I
caught a freight across the state line, and I'd been traveling
ever since . . . No, I didn't really hurt the guy. I've gotten a little rougher and tougher down through the years, but I've very
seldom really hurt anyone. I haven't had to.

I counted the money in my pocket, totting it up mentally
with the change I'd left on the bar. Four bucks. A little less
than four bucks. Maybe, I thought, maybe I ought to go
back. The doctors had thought I was making a little pro-
gress. I couldn't see it myself, but . . .

I guessed I wouldn't go back. I couldn't. The guy hadn't
seen me slug him, but what with me skipping out about
that time they probably knew I'd done it. And if I went
back they'd pin it on me. They wouldn't do it otherwise.
They probably wouldn't even report me missing. Unless a
guy is a maniac or a kind of big shot—someone in the public
eye, you know—he's very seldom reported. It's bad public-
ity for the institution, and anyway people usually aren't
interested.

I left the rest room, and went back to the bar. There was a

big station wagon parked in front of the door, and a woman was sitting on a stool near mine. She didn't look too good to me—not right then, she didn't. But that station wagon looked plenty good. I nodded to her politely and smiled in the mirror as I sat down.

"Rather a warm day," I said. "Really develops a person's thirst, doesn't it?"

She turned her head and looked at me. Taking her time about it. Looking me over very carefully from head to foot.

"Well, I'll tell you about that," she said. "If you're really interested in that, I'll give you my theory on the subject."

"Of course, I'm interested. I'd like to hear it."

"It's a pronoun," she said. "Also an adverb, conjunction and adjective."

She turned away, picking up her drink again. I picked up my beer my hand shaking a little.

"What a day," I said, kind of laughing to myself. "I was driving south with this friend of mine, Jack Billingsley—I guess you know the Billingsleys, big real estate family?—and our car stalled, and I walked back to a garage to get help. So I get back with the tow-truck, and darned if that crazy Jack isn't gone. I imagine what happened is—"

"—Jack got the car started himself," she said. "That's what happened. He started looking for you, and somehow you passed each other on the highway. Now he doesn't know where you are, and you don't know where he is."

She finished her drink, a double martini, and motioned to the bartender. He fixed her another one, giving me a long hard glare as he placed it in front of her.

"That darned crazy Jack," I said, laughing and shaking my head. "I wonder where in the world he can be. He ought to know I'd come in some place like this and wait for him."

"He probably had an accident," she said. "In fact, I think I read something about it."

"Huh? But you couldn't—"

"Uh-huh. He and a young lady called Jill. You read about it too, didn't you, Bert?"

"Yeah." The bartender kept on staring at me. "Yeah, I read about it. They're all wet, mister. They got their heads busted. I wouldn't wait around for 'em much longer, if I was you."

I played it dumb—kind of good-natured dumb. I said I certainly wasn't going to wait very much longer. "I think I'll have just one more beer, and if he hasn't shown up by then I'm going to go back to the city and catch a plane."

He slopped me out another beer. I started to drink it, my eyes beginning to burn, a hedged-in feeling creeping over me. They had my number, and hanging around wasn't going to make me a thing. But somehow I couldn't leave. I couldn't any more than I could have walked away from the Burlington Bearcat that night years ago. The Bearcat had been fouling me, too, giving it to me in the clinches, and calling me all kinds of dirty names. He'd kept it up—just like they were keeping it up. I couldn't walk away from him, just like I couldn't walk away from them, and I couldn't get him to stop, just like I couldn't get them to stop.

It came back with neonlike clarity. The lights were scorching my eyes. The resin dust, the beerish smell of ammonia, were strangling me. And above the roar of the crowd, I could hear that one wildly shrieking voice. "Stop him! Stop him! He's kicking his brains out! It's murder, MURDER!"

Now I raised my glass and took the rest of the beer at a gulp. I wished I could leave. I wished they'd lay off of me. And it didn't look like they would.

"Speaking of planes," she was saying. "I heard the funniest story about a man on a plane. Honestly, I just thought I'd die laughing when I—" She broke off, laughing, holding her handkerchief to her mouth.

"Why don't you tell it to him?" The bartender grinned, and jerked his head at me. "You'd like to hear a real funny story, wouldn't you, mister?"

"Why, yes. I always enjoy a good story."

"All right," she said, "this one will slay you. It seems there was an old man with a long gray beard, and he took the plane from Los Angeles to San Diego. The fare was fifteen dollars but he only had twelve, so they dropped him off at Oceanside."

I waited. She didn't say anything more. Finally, I said, "Yes, ma-am? I guess I don't get the point."

"Well, reach up on top of your head. Maybe you'll feel it."

They both grinned at me. The bartender jerked his thumb toward the door. "Okay, Mac. Disappear."

"But I haven't done anything, I've been acting all right. You've got no right to—"

"Beat it!" he snapped.

"I haven't asked you for anything," I said. "I came in here to wait for a friend, and I'm clean and respectable-looking and polite. And—and I'm an ex-serviceman and I've been to college—had a year and a half of college and—and—"

The veins in my throat were swelling. Everything began to look red and blurred and hazy.

I heard a voice, her voice, say, "Aah, take it easy, boy. Don't race your motor, kid." And from what I could see of her through the haze, she didn't look so bad. Now, she looked rather gentle and pretty—like someone you'd like to have for a friend.

The bartender was reaching across the counter for me. "Don't, Bert! Leave the guy alone!" she said, and then she let out a scream. Because he'd grabbed me by the shirt front, and when he did that I grabbed him. I locked an arm around his neck and dragged him halfway across the counter. I slugged him so hard it made my wrist ache.

I let go of him. He slid down behind the counter, and I ran.

2

It's funny how wrong your first impressions of people can be. Me, now, the first impression I'd had of her was that she wasn't much to look at—just a female barfly with money. And she *did* hit the booze too hard. Even I could see that. But I was all wrong about her looks. She was young. I'm thirty-three and she couldn't have been any older. She was pretty—beautiful, I should say—when she dolled herself up a little. She'd led a hard life for a long time, and it told on her face. But she had the looks, all right, the features and the figure. And sometimes—well, quite a bit of the time—she could act just as nice as she looked.

I'd only got down the road a few hundred yards when

the station wagon drew up beside me and she swung the door open. "Get in," she said, smiling. "It's all right. Bert isn't going to make any trouble for you."

"Yeah? Well, he's not going to get the chance, lady. I just stopped in there for a minute, and now I'm going on."

"I tell you it's all right. Bert's the last person in the world to holler for the cops. Anyway, we're not going back there. I'm taking you home with me."

"Home with you?" I said.

"It's not far from here." She patted the seat, smiling at me. "Come on, now. That's a good boy."

I got in rather uncertainly, wondering why she was acting so friendly now when she'd been so ornery a little while ago. She answered the question just as I started to ask it.

"I had a couple of reasons," she said. "For one thing, I didn't want Bert to know that I might be interested in you. The less a man like Bert knows about my business the better I like it."

"What else?"

"The other reason . . . well, I wanted to see what you would do; how nervy you were. Whether you were really the kind of guy I thought you might be."

I asked her what kind of guy that was exactly. She shrugged, a little impatiently.

"Oh, I don't know! Maybe . . . probably it doesn't make any difference, anyway."

The highway dipped down through a grove of trees with a narrow lane leading off to the south. She turned the car into the lane, and after about a quarter of a mile, just over the crest of a little hill, we came to her house.

It was a big white cottage standing in a clearing among several acres of trees. It looked like it might have been a nice place at one time. It still was fairly nice, but nothing like it could have been. The paint was peeling and dingy. Some of the front steps were caved in. Bricks from the chimney were scattered over the roof, and there were big rusted-out holes in some of the screens. The lawn didn't look like it had ever been cut. The grass was so high you could hardly see the sidewalks.

She sat looking out the window for a moment after we'd stopped. Then, she sighed and shook her head, murmuring something about work being the curse of the drinking classes.

"Well, here we are." She opened the door. "By the way, I'm Mrs. Anderson. Fay Anderson."

"I'm very happy to meet you, Mrs. Anderson."

"And I'm very happy to meet you. It's a unique privilege. I don't believe I've ever met a man before who didn't have a name."

"Oh, excuse me," I laughed. "I'm Bill Collins."

"No! Not *the* Bill Collins."

"Well, uh, I don't know. I guess maybe I am."

"Well, don't you feel bad about it. It's your story so you stick with it."

She was changing again, getting back to the orneriness. She was on and off like that all the time, I found out—nice to you one minute, needling you the next. It all depended upon how she felt, and how she felt depended upon how much booze she had in her. With just the right amount— and that changed, too, from hour to hour—she was nice. But if she didn't have it, if she had a little too much or not quite enough, she got mean.

"Well, come on!" she snapped. "What are you waiting for, anyway? Do you want me to carry you piggy-back?"

I hesitated, kind of fumbling around for something to say. She swore under her breath.

"Are you worried, Mr. Collins? Are you afraid I'll rob you of your money and valuables?"

I laughed and said, no, of course not. "I was just wondering . . . well, what about your husband? You said you were—"

"He won't rob you either. They only let him out of his grave on national holidays."

She slammed out of the car and flounced away a few steps, then she kind of got control of herself, I guess, and she came back.

"I've got a big steak in the refrigerator. I've got some cold beer and just about everything else in the beverage line. I've got some pretty good suits that belonged to my husband, and— But let it go. Do whatever you want to. Just say the word and I'll drive you back to the highway."

I said I wasn't in any particular hurry to get back to the

highway. "I was just wondering—I mean, what can I do for you?"

"How do I know?" Her voice went brittle again. "Probably nothing. What's the difference? Who are you to do anything for anyone?"

"Well, I guess I will come in for a little while."

We went in through the back door. She got busy in the kitchen fixing drinks, and I went on into the living room. Everything was kind of torn up and messy in there, like it was in the kitchen. The furniture was good—or rather it had been good—but there wasn't a whole lot of it. It looked incomplete, you know, like there might have been more at one time.

I kind of sauntered around, looking things over. I picked up some newspaper clippings from the sideboard and began to turn through them. They were all pictures of the same boy, a little seven-year-old youngster named Charles Vanderventer III. I tossed them back on the sideboard and sat down.

She came in with the drinks, bringing the bottle with her. While I was having one drink she had three.

"Bill Collins," she leaned back and looked at me. "Bill Collins. You know, I think I'll call you Collie."

"All right. A lot of people do call me Collie."

"That's because you look like one. Stupid and shaggy and with a big long nose to poke into other people's business. Just what was the idea in snooping around those clippings?"

"I wasn't snooping. They were just lying there so I picked them up and looked at them."

"Uh-huh. Oh, sure. Naturally."

"He's, uh, his family are friends of yours?" I was just making conversation; trying to steer her away from the orneriness. "You're related in some way?"

"He's my great-great grandson," she said. "One of the poorer branches of the family. I know you won't believe it, but they only have a paltry forty million dollars."

She poured another drink, filling her glass half full of whiskey. She leaned back again, face flushed, her narrowed black eyes sparkling with meanness.

"You're very fast with your mitts, Collie. Fast and

efficient. Did you ever fight professionally?"

"A little. A long time ago I had a few fights."

"What happened? Stop a few too many with your head?"

"There's nothing wrong with my head," I said. "I got out of it before there was anything wrong."

"And when did you get out of jail? The last time, that is."

I tried to keep smiling. I said that, well, as a matter of fact I had had a few brushes with the police. Just like any citizen would. Never anything serious. Just little misunderstandings and traffic tickets and so on.

"Oof!" She rolled her eyes. "Run for the hills, men!"

"I'll tell you something, Mrs. Anderson. I'd like to correct an erroneous impression you seem to have about me. I'm not at all stupid, Mrs. Anderson. I may sound like I am, but I'm really not."

"You'll have to swear to that, Collie. You give me your sworn statement, signed by two witnesses, and I'll take it under consideration."

"I'm not stupid. I don't like for people to treat me like I am. Most of my life I've been in— I've worked in places where it was hard to converse with anyone on an equal footing. It was hard to carry on an intelligent conversation, so I kind of lost the knack."

"Roger, Wilco. Collins coming in on the beam."

"I'm trying to explain something. Why don't you be polite and listen? I was saying that when you don't get to talk much, you get to where you sound kind of funny when you do talk. Kind of stilted and awkward, you know. You're not sure of yourself."

"Shut up!"

"But I—"

"Dammit, will you shut up? There's somebody coming!"

She jumped up and ran into the kitchen. I followed her. I watched as she opened the back door and stepped out onto the porch. It was getting dark now. The lights of a car swept over the trees and blinked out. The driver tapped out a shave-and-a-haircut on his horn.

Fay Anderson laughed and stayed down the steps.

"It's all right, Collie. It's just Uncle Bud."

"Uncle . . . Uncle Bud?"

"Fix yourself another drink. Fix three of them. We'll be in

in a minute."

It wasn't a minute. It was a lot nearer, I'd say, to thirty minutes. And I couldn't hear their conversation, of course, but I had a strong hunch that I was the subject of it.

I fixed three drinks, and drank them.

His real name was Stoker, Garret Stoker. He wasn't her uncle and I doubt that he was anyone's, but everyone called him Uncle Bud. He was a man of about forty, I think. He had snowy, prematurely gray hair, and warm friendly eyes, and a smile that made you feel good every time he turned it on. I don't know how she'd gotten acquainted with him, and probably she didn't either. Because that's the kind of a guy he was, if you know what I mean. You meet guys like Uncle Bud once—just over a drink or a cup of coffee—and you feel like you've known them all your life. They make you feel that way.

The first thing you know they're writing down your address and telephone number, and the next thing you know they're dropping around to see you or giving you a ring. Just being friendly, you understand. Not because they want anything. Sooner or later, of course, they want something; and when they do it's awfully hard to say no to them. No matter what it is. Even when it's like something *this* Uncle Bud wanted.

He wrung my hand, and said it was a great pleasure to meet me. Then, still hanging onto my hand, giving it a little squeeze now and then, he turned around to Fay.

"I just can't understand it, Fay. I still believe you're joking with me. Why, I'd have bet money that there wasn't a man, woman or child in the United States who hadn't heard of Kid Collins."

"Bet me some money," she said. "I'll give you seven to five."

"Well . . ." He laughed and released my hand. "Ain't this little lady a case, Kid? Never serious for a moment. But she's true-blue, understand, a real little pal, and the kidding's all in fun. She don't mean a thing by it."

"Yes, sir, I understand."

"Let's see, now. When was that last fight of yours, the big one? Wasn't it in, uh—?

"It—it was in 1940. The Burlington Bearcat. He was—" My voice trailed away. "I mean it wasn't a very big fight, sir."

"Sure sure. A preliminary bout. But it was still a mighty big fight. Uh, it was in—I was arguing with a fellow about it the other day, and he claimed it was held in Newark. I said it was in, uh—"

"It was in Detroit," I said.

"That's right. That's exactly right!" he exclaimed. "Detroit, 1940, a four-round prelim. What did I tell you Fay? Didn't I tell you I knew the Kid's record backwards and forwards?"

Fay groaned and slapped herself on the forehead. Uncle Bud winked at me, and I grinned and winked back at him.

I began to like him a lot.

Fay said that if we wanted any dinner, we could darned well fix it ourselves. So that's what we did. Uncle Bud pounded the steak and put it on to broil, and I peeled and sliced potatoes. He opened some cans of peas and apple sauce, and I made coffee and ice water.

"Well, Kid," he said, while we were waiting for the stuff to cook, "I'm glad you've decided to settle down for a while. Now, that you've found friends—people who admire you and really take an interest in you—"

"Settle down?" I blinked. "Settle down where?"

"Why right here—where else?" he said firmly. "Our little lady kind of needs someone to keep an eye on her, and there's a nice little apartment out over the garage. Yes, sir, you just move right in, Kid. Just take it easy for a few days. Get rested up and keep Fay out of trouble and I'll see what I can stir up for you. I got an idea that I might be able to put you next to something pretty good."

He nodded to me, giving the steak a turn.

I said, maybe he already had his eye on something he could put me next to.

"Sharp." He laughed. "I told Fay you were. I said, 'Now, Fay, maybe the guy's had a rough time, but if that's Kid

Collins you've got with you, he's nobody's fool. He's nervy and he's sharp,' I said. 'He'll know a good angle when he sees one and he'll have what it takes to carry through on it. And you treat him right, and he'll treat you right.' "

"Look, sir. Look, Uncle Bud . . ."

"Yeah, Kid? Go right ahead and get it off your chest."

"Well, I appreciate your kindness, the compliments and all, but—but you don't really know anything about me. You couldn't. You're just trying to be nice, and probably if you really knew the kind of guy I was, you wouldn't feel like this."

"I'll tell you what I know, I know people, Kid. I know what they'll do and what they won't. Or, put it another way, what they can do and what they can't. I was a city detective here for years—maybe Fay told you? Well, I was, and I was able to put a lot of bright boys next to some pretty good things. Some of them had played an angle before, but most of 'em hadn't. They'd never turned a trick—didn't think they could—until I showed them the way."

"And you're not a detective, now?"

He glanced around sharply, frowning at me for the first time. Then, he pursed his lips and went back to stirring the potatoes.

"We'll have to see," he said absently. "We'll have to get better acquainted. I think you'd be just right—smart enough, but not too . . ."

"Yes?" I said.

"Never mind, Kid." His smile came back. "There's no rush. It's something we'll have to take our time on."

We ate dinner; he and I did, rather. Fay came to the table, but she didn't really eat anything. She just sat there—mussing the food on her plate, drinking and sniping at us every time we opened our mouths.

"This damned house," she said, glaring at Uncle Bud. "I thought you were going to turn it in for me right away. I thought you were going to make me a nice little profit on it. You talked me into buying the damned dump, and then you—"

"Now, Fay," he said, calmly. "You'll do all right on it. You'll make out—one way or another."

"Oh, yeah?" Her eyes wavered. "And what about that

lousy station wagon? I tie up practically the last nickel I got in the thing, and you—"

"Now, Fay. You know I got you a good deal on it. You know you need a good car living out here."

"Who the hell wants to live out here?" She almost yelled it. "Who the hell talked me into it?"

"You'll thank me for it. You just trust your old Uncle Bud, and you'll be wearing diamonds."

He turned the conversation to me, asked me what I'd been doing since I quit fighting. I said I'd been in the army for a while right after I quit, and I'd just been knocking around since then.

"The army, huh? Get along all right?"

"Why, pretty good. I thought I did, anyway."

Fay laughed. Uncle Bud frowned and shook his head at her.

"I did the best I could," I said. "But they weren't very patient, and it kind of looked like they were trying to see how tough they could make things on me. So, well, I landed in the brig a few times, and finally they sent me to the hospital. And right after that they let me go."

"Mmm-hmm." He nodded thoughtfully. "You were, uh, all right then? Just, uh, just couldn't adjust to the military life. Well, that's not unusual. I understand that there were any number of men who had that kind of trouble."

Fay laughed again and Uncle Bud gave her another shake of his head.

"Sure," he said, softly. "I understand how it was, Kid. It's that way all through life, it seems like. People expecting a guy to get along with them, but they won't try to get along with him. Maybe he just needs a little help, just a little understanding, but ninety-nine times out of a hundred he won't get it."

I said I wouldn't want him to get the idea that there was anything wrong with me. There really wasn't much wrong with me, you know—not then, there wasn't—and I felt that I had to say it. Because if there's one thing that scares people, it's mental trouble.

You can be an ex-convict, even a murderer, say, and maybe it won't bother 'em a bit. They'll give you a job, take you into their homes, make friends with you. But if you've got any kind of mental trouble, or if you've ever had any, well, that's another story. They're afraid of you. They want no part of you.

Uncle Bud seemed to believe what I told him. The way he had me sized up, I guess, was as a guy who hadn't been too bright to begin with and had got just a shade punchy in the ring.

"Sure, you're okay, Kid. All you need is some dough, enough so's you can take life easy and not have to worry."

"Yeah. But . . . well, I guess I ought to tell you something else, too, Uncle Bud. I've—I've always tried to do the right thing. Never anything really bad or—"

"Oh, well." He spread his hands. "What do the words mean, Kid? What's good and what's bad? Now, I'd say it was bad for a nice guy like you to have to go on like he's been going. I'd say it would be good if you never had to worry about money for the rest of your life."

"Yeah, I guess it would be."

"Naturally. Naturally, you wouldn't want to hurt anyone. You wouldn't have to. It would just be a case of putting pressure on certain people—people that have more dough than they know what to do with—and making 'em come across. That would be all right, wouldn't it?"

I hesitated. "Well, it sounds—"

And Fay slammed her glass down on the table.

"It sounds rotten!" she yelled at Uncle Bud. "It sounds terrible, filthy, lousy! I don't know why I ever—I won't have any part of it, understand? You may talk Stupid here into it, b-but you can go ahead without me, and I w-won't—"

She stumbled to her feet, crying, and staggered out of the room. Uncle Bud raised his eyebrows at me.

"Poor little lady. But she'll snap out of it. Now, why don't you and I do these dishes, and then I'll run along."

We cleared up the dishes. I tried to talk to him while we were working, trying to get something more out of him about this proposition he had in mind. But he kept changing the subject, his voice getting shorter and shorter. And finally he turned on me, half-snarling, and told me to drop it.

"Forget it! I'll tell you whatever you need to know, when you need to know it!"

He glared at me, his eyes kind of glazed. And I was too startled to say anything back to him. I'd thought he was such an easy-going, good-natured guy, and now he looked like some sort of vicious, mean-tempered animal.

"I'll tell you something else, too." He tapped me on the chest. "I ain't just kidding about you sleeping in the garage. That's where you sleep, get me, and you sleep by yourself. You don't make no play for the little lady."

I nodded, feeling kind of hurt and embarrassed. I guessed I had stared at her quite a bit that evening, but I hadn't meant anything by it. I didn't have the slightest idea of trying to take advantage of her.

"Maybe I'd better clear out. If you think I'm that kind of guy, I wouldn't want to stick around."

"Aw, now, don't take it that way," he said soothingly. And suddenly he was his old self again. "You'll have to excuse me, Kid. Just forget I said anything. I've had a pretty hard day, and I spoke without thinking."

I walked out to the car with him. We shook hands, and he said not to worry about a thing, just to take it easy and he'd be out to see me the next day. He left then, and I went back into the house. And, of course, I didn't feel very easy. I couldn't help but worry.

I fixed myself a couple of drinks. They kind of eased me down a little, so I fixed another one. I sauntered over to the sideboard with it, and picked up the newspaper clippings again. I thumbed through them absently, wondering why they were there and why Fay'd had me come here—and suddenly I stopped wondering. Suddenly I knew why. I didn't know the how of it, the details, but I knew what it was all about.

I dropped the clippings, as though they'd all at once caught fire. I turned back around, and there she was, just coming out of the bedroom. She was pale and sick-looking, but she seemed fairly sober. She sat down and reached for the bottle, smiling at me in a kind of tired, taunting way.

"Well, Collie?" she said. "Well, my blushing boy, my beamish friend?"

"Well, what?"

"You really don't know?" She poured a big drink of whiskey. "You've been slapped in the face with a polecat and you still can't smell anything?"

I shrugged. She drained her glass, and reached for the bottle again.

"Sure, you know." She nodded. "This house and a crooked ex-cop and those pictures, and—and you. Even you could add that one up."

"About that crooked ex-cop. About him . . . and you. He sort of acts like—I mean he said a thing or two to me that—"

"Yes? Well, that's one thing you *don't* need to worry about. There's nothing between us. There isn't going to be anything."

"I don't think he looks at it that way. It's none of my business, of course."

"Right. So let's get back to something that is. Listen closely to Old Mother Anderson, and then get the hell out. Because I'm only laying it on the line for you once . . . A chump is required, Collie. A Grade-A hundred-proof sucker. Someone with a barrel of nerve and a pint of brains. Does that description fit anyone of your acquaintance?"

"I wouldn't care to say. It might partly fit certain people I've met. Women who drink too much and talk while they're drinking."

"Boing!" She triggered a finger at her forehead. "But I'm my own chump, Collie. Strictly my own. Oh, I do an occasional benefit performance, but, by and large and on the whole, to coin a phrase—correction: two phrases—"

"I thought you were going to tell me something. You make a big production out of it, and then you don't say anything."

"I'll tell you something. This. All you need to know, Collie. If he thought you were half-way bright, Uncle Bud wouldn't want you. He's not too sharp himself—if he was he'd still be on the force—and he won't play with anyone who is."

"Including you?"

"Forget about me. I don't count—and you can sing that to any tune you like."

"I guess I don't understand," I said. "You picked me up today. You brought me here to meet Uncle Bud. You do all that, and then, after I'm half-way in, you—"

"It's confusing, isn't it? Why not just say that I'm a cuh-razy, mixed-up neurotic. Or we might say that occasionally—just occasionally now—I feel a twinge of decency." She took a swig straight from the bottle, and the whiskey trickled down over her chin. "Get out, Collie. This little frammis has been cooking for months, and if you leave it'll go right on cooking until it boils away. Nothing will happen without you. No one else would be chump enough to touch it."

"Well," I said. "I guess . . ." And then something happened inside my head, and I left the sentence unfinished. It was as though I'd been walking in my sleep and suddenly waked up.

Kidnaping? Me, a *kidnaper?* Why was I arguing with her? What in hell had come over me? I'd never done anything really bad. Just the things a man like me has to do to stay alive. Yet now, just since this afternoon, I was . . . I pushed myself to my feet, feeling dizzy and sick. Everything was kind of blurred for a minute. "That's my good boy, that's my Collie darling," I heard her say. "Just a minute, honey."

She hurried into her bedroom, and came back with her purse. She took out a small roll of bills, stripped off one of them and squeezed the rest into my hand.

"I'd ask you to stay tonight, Collie, if it wasn't for Uncle Bud. I don't want him talking you into this mess, and if he saw you before you got away—"

"I know. I'd better go now."

"Take the bottle with you. You look lonely, and a bottle can be a lot of company."

She stood on tiptoe and kissed me; and afterwards she leaned against me for a moment, her head against my chest. She made a mighty nice armful, all warmness and fullness and sweet-smelling softness. I brushed her thick black hair with my lips, and she sighed and shivered. And moved out of my arms.

"What about you? What's going to happen to you, Fay?"

"Nothing. The same thing that's been happening since my husband died."

"But I thought there was something, some organization or treatment that could help you."

"There is, but not for what ails me. They haven't found that yet. When you've leaned on someone all your life, been completely dependent upon him and never made a decision of your own. And when he's suddenly taken away— Oh, n-never mind, Collie. Just go and keep going."

She turned on the porchlight for me so I could find my way across the yard. Where the lane entered the trees, I turned around and waved.

The lights went off. If she waved back, I didn't see her. Everything was dark, and she and the house were gone. As though they had never existed. I felt kind of sad in a way, but at the same time I felt good.

I picked my way down the lane, taking a sip from the bottle now and then. A couple of times I stumbled and fell down, but it didn't bother me much. And it didn't seem dark, but light.

I'd been in the dark, a nightmare. I'd almost been trapped in one. But now I'd waked up and got away, and it was light again. I'd seen my last of that place, I thought. It was gone away, vanished into the darkness. I'd never been there, and it had never been there.

But it was there. I hadn't seen the last of it.

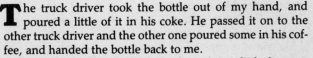

The truck driver took the bottle out of my hand, and poured a little of it in his coke. He passed it on to the other truck driver and the other one poured some in his coffee, and handed the bottle back to me.

The counterman watched us, frowning a little but not really sore. He'd taken a couple of drinks, too, and he was just worried, not sore.

"Don't flash the jug around so much, huh?" he said. "Some highway patrolman comes by here, he might make trouble."

"Aaah!" One of the truck drivers winked at him. "Why would anyone make trouble for Collie? Collie's just waiting for a streetcar."

"Not a streetcar. I'm waiting for this friend of mine, Jack

Billingsley. You see—"

"Sure." The other truck driver grinned. "What kind of plane did you say he was flying?"

"I've told you several times now," I said. "It's an automobile. It—"

"Oh, yeah. A Rolls-Royce, wasn't it?"

"No, he's got a Rolls-Royce—two of them, in fact—but he wasn't driving one today. What he had today was a big Cadillac convertible. Some little thing went wrong with it, so I started walking back to a garage—"

"Maybe he had to stop to feed the horses . . ."

"Maybe the caboose ran off the track . . ."

"Maybe," I said, "a couple of wise guys would like to have their faces pushed in."

The lunchroom went dead silent. The truck drivers stopped grinning, and the counterman glanced uneasily toward the telephone. After a moment I forced a laugh.

"I'm only joking, of course. We're all here joking and drinking together, so I joked a little too. I didn't mean it any more than you meant the things you said to me."

One of the truck drivers laid some change on the counter. He and the other one got up, and kind of edged toward the door. I stood up too.

"How about a ride?" I said. "I've got a little money, and there's still some of the whiskey left."

"Sorry. Company says no riders."

"I can ride in the back. Just let me ride with you until daylight. Maybe not even until daylight. I'll probably see that darned crazy Jack Billingsley on the road."

The screen door slammed, then the truck doors. The motor roared, and they were gone. The counterman stared at me. I stared back at him. Finally his eyes wavered and he spoke sort of whining.

"Please, Mac. Clear out, will you, huh? You ain't never going to get no ride."

"I certainly won't get one out on the highway. No one'll stop for me at night."

"But that ain't my fault! You got no right hanging around here, getting me into trouble. What'll people think, for gosh sake? They come in here, an' you start jabbering away at 'em . . ."

"I'm sorry. I won't say another word to anyone. I'll just wait around quietly until it gets a little lighter."

He groaned and cursed under his breath. "Well, get away from the counter then! If you simply got to hang around, go an' set in that rear booth."

"Why, certainly. I'll be glad to."

I went back to the rear booth. I slid in as close as I could to the wall and put my head down on my arms. I was worn out, what with all I'd been through and not being in a bed for three days. But I couldn't relax, let alone sleep. My mind kept going back to Fay—how nice she'd been to me, and what was going to happen to her. I couldn't rest or relax.

I sat up and lighted a cigarette. I took a couple more drinks, and put my head down again. Finally I dozed. Or, I guess I should say, I passed out.

I came out of it frightened, not knowing where I was, not remembering how I had got here. I jumped up almost before my eyes were open, and headed for the door.

The bottle slid out of my pocket. I made a grab for it, and it sort of jumped out of my hands. It bounced and rolled along the floor, and I stumbled after it, staggering and bumping into the other booths until I finally fell down in one.

There was a man in it, a customer, sitting on the bench opposite me. A young-oldish looking fellow, or maybe you could call him old-youngish looking. He glanced at the counterman and shook his head. Then he stooped down and picked up the bottle. He handed it to me, picking up the sandwich he'd been eating.

"Pretty good." He motioned with it casually. "Like to have me order you one?"

"No, thank you."

"I think you should. Have some coffee anyway."

I said, thank you; I guessed I'd wait to eat until my friend, Jack Billingsley, showed up. "That darned crazy Jack." I laughed. "We were on our way to California, driving at night, you know, because it's so much cooler. And . . ."

He went on eating, keeping his eyes on his plate. Then, suddenly he looked up. He listened, frowning, staring into my eyes and studying my face.

"All right . . ." He laid a hand on my arm gently. "No harm done. It's a nice harmless little story and shows a fine imagination, but it's not necessary with me. Where do you live?"

"Well . . ."

"I see. Been getting along all right?"

"About like always. Pretty good, I guess. Not really good, you know, but all right."

"How long since you were under commitment?"

I started to say a few days, but then I changed it real fast. I said it had been over a year. The name of the place I gave him was the one before the last one.

"Would you like to go back to it? Don't you think you should go back?"

"Well, I guess I should, kind of. I haven't been in trouble or anything, but— You're a doctor?"

"Yes. And I think you should go back, too. Unless, of course, you've got some friend or member of your family who can help you."

"I haven't."

"Well, let's see . . ." He rubbed his face. "Let's see, now. I wonder what you'd better—" He broke off scowling, looking sort of mad at himself. "I'll tell you—what's your name, Collins? Well, I'll tell you, Collins, you'd better take whatever money you can get together and go straight back."

"Yes, sir. I'll do that. I can probably hitchhike most of the way."

"I wish I could help you myself, but I just don't have the time and the money. I can only do so much, and I'm already—"

"I'll tell you what I might do," I broke in. "Maybe I could get a commitment in this state."

"A non-resident?" He laughed briefly. "Not that it would mean much if you were resident. Sometimes, Collins, sometimes I think they take them in the front door here and lead them right on out the back."

"Yes, sir. I guess it's pretty much that way everywhere."

"They can't get the money to operate on. There's money for highways and swimming pools and football stadiums. For everything but the most important things. And then people wonder. They wonder why, when some terrible tragedy takes place, that—"

"I'll be all right," I assured him. "You don't need to worry about me, Doctor."

"Well." He bit his lip. "Well, here. Let me give you my card, anyway. If you should remain in this section, and if there's any kind of emergency—even if it isn't an emergency, if you just want to talk to someone—why, be sure to call me."

I thanked him, and said I'd certainly do that. He slid out of the booth, walked over to the counter, and paid his check.

He started toward the door. Then he wheeled around abruptly and came back to the booth.

"You're sure you'll be all right, Collins? You'll lay off the booze, and, uh, behave yourself?"

"Yes, sir."

"Fine. Good boy. You go back there and stay this time. Stay no matter how long it takes."

"Yes, sir. That's just what I'm going to do, Doctor."

He kind of sighed and shook his head. "You are like hell! How can you? Why the hell should you? Come on!"

"What?" I said. "Come on?"

"And make it snappy, dammit. Before I have time to change my mind."

He lived in the city, the one I'd passed through that morning. He had a nice little brick cottage there, just inside the city limits, with his offices in the front and his living quarters in the rear. Except that I kept thinking about Fay Anderson—and worrying about her—the three days I spent there were just about the most pleasant I can remember.

There were plenty of books to read. There was a big lawn I could work on whenever I got restless, lots of food in the refrigerator, and a bedroom all of my own. I think I enjoyed that last more than anything else. Most places I'd been in— you know, "places"—I was always crowded. There'd maybe be a dozen of us in one little room. You looked around, and they'd be watching you. They looked around, and you'd be watching them. And you never got used to it.

The longer it went on, the more it bothered you. It would have been bad enough if you were all the same kind of guys and had the same degree of mental disturbance, but you just never were. Just when you thought you had a pretty good gang, they'd move in someone that was honest-to-gosh *bad*. A real wild-eyed guy—just anyone, it looked like, that could get around without a strait jacket. And before long you began to feel a little wild-eyed yourself. You couldn't rest. How can you rest when there's some lunatic in the same room with you?

There at Doc's house, in a big room all of my own, I really slept for the first time in years. I didn't have any medication after the first night. I didn't want any, and Doc said I didn't need any.

The third night—well, it was actually the fourth—he came in and sat down on the edge of my bed. He asked me how I was feeling, and I said I'd never felt better. He murmured that that was good, to get all the rest I could so I'd be in good shape for my trip.

"Of course," he said, not looking at me, "you'll probably be here several weeks yet. Perhaps several months. I sent the institution a wire three days ago, but these things take a lot of time."

"Yes," I agreed. "I don't know why they should, but I guess they do."

"I was going to ask you, Collie." He kept his eyes away from mine. "In case, they should refuse to send for you; if they don't feel able to, that is, because of the expense . . ."

"Yes, Doc?"

"How would you feel about staying on here with me? There's plenty you could do to earn your keep. Yard work and car repairs and so on. You'd be a big help to me, and I think I'd be of some help to you, and— Well, it would be a fine arrangement for both of us. What do you say, Collie? Would you like to do that?"

"I—I— Excuse me just a minute. Doc. I'll be right back."

I got up and went into the bathroom. I stayed in there with the door closed until I was sure I could control myself.

Good old Doc, I thought. He was a swell guy, but he was just about the world's worst liar. He'd had plenty of time to hear from the institutional authorities in that state where I'd been. I knew that he had heard from them, too, and that they had refused to send for me. I'd been almost sure that they would. They'll very seldom send for a guy unless he's a violent or criminal case.

Now, since there was no one else to look after me, Doc was willing to take on the job himself. I washed my face, and ran a drink of water. Then I made myself smile, and went back into the bedroom again. I said that I'd be tickled to death to stay. I tried to look natural and sound natural, but I guess it wasn't a perfect try.

"I can afford it, Collie." He looked at me closely, and looked away again. "Why, I'd tell you so in a minute if I couldn't."

"Fine."

"It's all settled then? You'll stay?"

"As long as you can afford it."

"I can. I want you to and you must. You see, Collie, your judgment just isn't good. You're inherently decent with a lot of good, strong moral fibre, but that isn't enough. There'll come a time or a situation when it won't be enough. A man in your condition is readily influenced by others; broadly speaking, he has to depend on them. And you and I know they're not always dependable . . ."

He paused and lit his pipe. He took a few puffs on it, then went on again.

"Sometimes they're merely ignorant. Sometimes they're cruel or criminal. In any case, they're playing with dynamite. Actually, Collie, there'd be much less danger in your roaming around on your own if you were an out-and-out lunatic—one of the wild-eyed guys, to borrow your own expression. People could *see* the danger then. Now, well, what do they see, now? Why, they see an unusually handsome young man. A little eccentric perhaps, a little slow on the uptake occasionally, but in most respects normal. So they treat you as though you were normal, and the result sooner or later, is certain to be tragedy. For you, for others. You only need to look at almost any daily newspaper to see that I'm right."

"I don't know, Doc, I've been pretty good about steering clear of trouble. I've never hurt anyone or ever done anything really bad."

"What do you call really bad, Collie? And how do you take it when someone kids you or teases you? Never mind."

He smiled and slapped me on the knee. "I'm sure you've done fine, hard as it was. And from now on you'll do even better. You stay here for a year or so, however long it takes, and . . ."

He left on his calls around ten the next morning. As soon as he was gone, I called the doctors' answering service and reported him out.

Then, I left too.

Fay Anderson had given me about thirty dollars when I left her place, and I'd had around three of my own. But, now, I had a little less than five. I don't know what had happened to the rest of it, whether I'd jerked it out of my pocket and lost it or whether someone had gotten it away from me in that lunchroom. But that little bit, around five dollars, was all I had left.

It was almost worse than having nothing.

I couldn't really travel anywhere on it. It wasn't more than enough to live on a day or so. A few days before, five dollars would have looked pretty good to me. But I'd kind of changed since then. I didn't see how I could go back to living like I had—knocking around and getting knocked around. Sleeping in culverts and begging for handouts, and bumming rides to places I didn't actually care about going to.

As Uncle Bud said, that was bad. Really bad. When I thought about it, certain other things didn't look so bad at all.

I used fifteen cents of my money for a crosstown bus fare. I got off at the highway, the one that led past her place, and, well, for a while, I just loafed around there. I sat on the bus-stop bench, and I got an ice cream cone from a peddler, and I window-shopped the neighborhood stores. It was hard to decide what to do. I always have trouble making decisions, and this was a particularly hard one.

I paced back and forth in front of the store windows, arguing with myself, fumbling with that little bit of money I had in my pockets. I certainly didn't want to put Fay on the spot, more or less force her to go ahead with something she was against. On the other hand, she was already on a pretty bad spot, wasn't she? She couldn't go on like that, anymore than I could go on like this. And it would be good to see her again. So I could just stop by for a visit, couldn't I? I wouldn't need to stay.

It was when I was looking in a liquor store window that I finally made up my mind. There was a big curved-neck bottle inside—just wine, but it looked mighty fancy, and the price was only three ninety-eight. I figured it would make a nice present for her. I could take that out to her, and it would give me a reason for stopping by.

I bought it. Then, I stepped out on the highway and started thumbing. No one would stop for me, but finally a truck came by slow enough so I could hop on the tailgate.

It was pretty rough riding there, and the day was another scorcher. I kept jouncing up and down, and, of course, the wine did too. And I imagine it got a lot hotter than I did.

We came to the little lane that led up to her house. I swung off the truck, running, and that final jouncing was just a little bit more than the wine could take. The bottle exploded; it blew up right in my arms. There must have been a gallon of that sticky red wine, and I'll bet every drop of it went on me.

I hated to call on Fay looking that way, but I didn't have any choice. I had to get washed up and do something about my clothes, and her house was the only place I could.

It was early in the afternoon when I got there. She'd only been up a couple hours, so she hadn't had too much to drink. Quite a lot for the average person, I suppose, but not for Fay. It was just enough to put her in a good mood.

"Oh, Collie! You crazy, silly, sweet—" She threw her arms around me, laughing. "What in the world happened to you, baby?"

"Well, I just happened to be in the neighborhood. I thought I'd bring you a little present, a little wine."

"A barrel, darling? Were you rolling it across—" she laughed uproariously—"across the highway and through the trees to Grandma's house?"

She laughed and laughed, kind of crying along with it. She pushed me into a chair, and sat down on my lap. And I tried to tell her she'd get all messy, but she didn't even seem to hear me.

"I'm glad you came back, Collie," she whispered. "I wish you hadn't, I prayed that you wouldn't, Collie. But I'm glad."

"I'm glad, too. I didn't mean to, but it just seemed like I had to. After I met you and . . . and everything, I just couldn't take that old concrete pasture any more."

"The—the what, Collie?"

"The concrete pasture. I mean, that's what it seems like to me. You keep going and going, and it's always the same everywhere. Wherever you've been, wherever you go, everywhere you look. Just grayness and hardness, as far as you can see."

"I know. I know what you mean." She shivered and kissed me. "But this other . . . It seems like there should be some other way."

"I guess there probably is. There's probably lots of other ways. But no one's ever pointed them out to me, and I've never been able to find them for myself."

"Poor Collie. Have you had a hard time these last few days, darling? Where have you been?"

"Nowhere. Just fooling around."

I took a bath and put on some clothes she gave me. We had lunch, and then we talked some more.

At first she said we'd find another way out. There was bound to be another way and we'd find it. When Uncle Bud showed up we'd toss him out on his ear. But she was drinking while she was talking and she kept tossing the booze down. So it wasn't long before the good mood was gone, and she'd completely reversed herself.

"Collie, Collie, the wonder souphound. Why don't you dig us up some bones, boy? Dig us a cave to live in."

"You shouldn't say things like that, Fay. I know you don't mean it."

"There in the bar that day. You thought you were hooking into a soft touch, didn't you? You thought you could take me for everything I had. Well, you can so why don't you? Take the damned car and the damned house, and see what you can do with 'em! Of course, you'll have to pay off a couple of little mortgages first."

"Maybe I could," I said. "I mean, maybe if we had a little money, and I could get some kind of a job . . ."

"You jerk! You imbecile. What kind of job could you hold—hunting sand in the Sahara?"

A blinding pain stabbed through my forehead. I said that if that was the way she felt about me; I'd better clear out.

"Well, why the hell don't you?" she yelled. "Do it and stop talking about it!"

She staggered into the bedroom, slamming the door behind her. I got up and went out to the back porch. And, then, after a minute or two, I started down the lane toward the highway.

It was the best thing to do, I figured; the only thing to do. Because if she acted this way now, when she didn't know there was really anything wrong with me, how would she act if she knew the truth? A lot of normal people are scared to death of anyone with mental trouble. And with those booze-shot nerves of hers, she was a long ways from being normal. Probably she wouldn't say anything, do anything openly. She'd be too scared. But she wouldn't want any part of me—she wouldn't, and Uncle Bud wouldn't. And yet if I was tied up with them in a kidnaping, if I knew something about them that might send them to the chair . . .

Well, you see what I mean. They'd feel that they had to get rid of me. They might not like to do it—at least, Fay might not—but they'd think that they had to and they would.

Anyway, that's the way things looked to me just then.

I was almost to the highway when Uncle Bud's car turned into the lane, He came to a quick stop and leaned out. I gave him a grunt and a nod, and kept on going.

"Wait a minute, Kid!" He jumped out and caught me by the arm. "This is a way to treat a pal, Kid? I've been laying awake nights worrying about you and hoping you'd come back, and then the minute I see you—"

"I'm in a hurry." I cut him off. "I just stopped at the house to tell Fay good-bye, and now I'm on my way again."

"Naw. No, you're not, Kid!" he said firmly. "I ain't letting you pass up a deal as sweet as this. You hop right in the car, and whatever's bothering you, we'll— You ain't sore at me, are you? I didn't hurt your feelings with that little joke I made about sleeping by yourself?"

He looked up at me anxiously, his face all friendly concern. I said that it hadn't sounded like much of a joke to me.

"So I just wasn't thinking!" he said. "So—" he laughed uncomfortably—"so maybe it wasn't a joke. Maybe I don't like the idea of another guy making time with Fay when I've never been able to get to first base."

"Well, I wasn't trying anything like that."

"Sure, you weren't, But if you do try to, Kid—if you want to and she wants to—you'll never hear another peep out of me. I need you too much, know what I mean? I've been looking for a guy like you for months, and now that I've found you—"

"I think you'd better count me out. I—I don't seem to get along too well with Fay."

"Aah, sure you do!" He clapped me on the back. "She was needling you, huh? Well, don't you mind her at all, because she don't mean a thing in the world by it."

"But there's something else." I hesitated. "Something about me . . ."

"So you've had a little trouble." He shrugged. "Who the hell hasn't? Now pile into the car, and forget this stuff about clearing out."

I knew it was all wrong. He had to have me, so he was willing to forget about Fay for a while. But as soon as he was through with me—or if something made him decide that I *wasn't* any use to him . . .

It was all wrong any way you looked at it. Fay in the shape she was in. And me in my condition. And Uncle Bud feeling like he did about me. And the kidnaping itself. Kidnaping—the dirtiest kind of crime there is. Still, it was either this or nothing, the way things looked to me. It was either this, or the old concrete pasture. So I got into the car with him and went back to the house. I wanted to believe that things would turn out all right, so I went back. And inside of an hour I was back up on top of the world again.

Everything was fine. Everything was going to be finer. Uncle Bud knew it and he made me know it.

He didn't try to kid me that the job wouldn't be dangerous. But once it was pulled, we'd be safe and we were a cinch for the dough. We'd be able to duck the traps that kidnapers are usually caught in. We'd know about them in advance, whether the ransom bills were marked or registered, or whether there was a police stake-out at the payoff place. Uncle Bud still had all kinds of contacts inside of the department. He'd know every move that was being made, before it was made. So there might be traps, but they wouldn't catch anyone.

We'd get the money, a quarter of a million dollars, and we'd get away with it.

We didn't discuss the actual kidnaping that evening. Uncle Bud said we'd take that up after I got settled down a bit. I didn't argue with him. I was feeling good. Whatever there was to worry about—and I guessed there was probably plenty—I didn't want to face up to it just then.

Fay waked up. She got to feeling fairly good again, and the three of us went out to the garage apartment. We dusted it out, put clean sheets on the bed, and so on. Then we went back to the house, and after a while Fay began to razz me a little. But she was more funny about it than mean, so I didn't really mind.

Uncle Bud left around ten o'clock. Or, I should say, he started to. He was telling me good night, shaking hands with me, when he turned suddenly and looked out the window.

"Somebody's coming! Get that light off! Get out of sight, Kid! Fay . . ."

Fay hurried to the window and looked out. She stood there a moment, peering through the glass. I heard a car door slam.

"You'd better go into the bedroom, Collie. Take your glass with you. But it's all right for Uncle Bud to stay." She turned around. "It's only Bert."

"Bert!" Uncle Bud turned white. "You mean that character from the roadhouse? Hell, if he sees me . . ."

"What's the difference? He can't tie you in with anything."

"He's threatened to kill me! We were in on a deal together, and he thinks—" He broke off frantically, snatching up his glass. "Don't let on I'm here, understand? There ain't no one here but you!"

"But your car! What'll I tell him?"

"He doesn't know my car when he sees it! Tell him—tell him it broke down on the highway and the people pushed it in here for the night!"

I was already in her bedroom. He beat it in after me, leaving the door cracked open a little. He was really scared. I could hear him panting in the darkness, hear the nervous rattle of papers in his pockets. Whatever he'd pulled on Bert, it must have been pretty raw.

Bert only came in as far as the kitchen, so we couldn't hear everything that was said. But from what we could hear, it sounded like a purely social call. Fay was a good customer of his. She hadn't been into his place for several days, and he'd wanted to see if she was all right.

He left after a few minutes. Uncle Bud followed me out of the bedroom, wiping the sweat from his face.

"Boy," he said shakily. "Was that a close one!"

"Mmm," said Fay. "So it would seem. Just what kind of swindle did you work on him, anyway?"

"None, Nothing." Uncle Bud shook his head fretfully. "Bert's just plain unreasonable, know what I mean? You try to explain something to him, show him exactly why a proposition went wrong and it isn't your fault, and he won't even listen. He just holds his hand out, and tells you to come across."

Fay yawned and sat down again. She looked at me, that mean sparkle coming into her eyes.

"Well, Collie, what do you think of our head man, the genius who's going to lead us safely from rags to riches? A truly great mind, wouldn't you say? Of course, it may get him killed, but at least he did manage to swindle a barkeep."

Uncle Bud laughed and gave me a nudge. He said I wasn't to pay Fay any mind, because she was just the world's greatest little kidder. "But look, Fay," he added, "it ain't going to do for that character to be dropping by here. If it should happen later on, after we—"

"Forget it!" Fay snapped. "That was Bert's first visit here in months, and I'll see that it's his last. I've got a strong stomach, but one bird like you is about all I can take."

Uncle Bud laughed again. He was after something, you see, and he wasn't going to let himself be insulted until he'd got it. He left a few minutes later. Fay and I talked for a while longer, after he'd gone. Or, I should say, I tried to talk to her. Because I didn't have much luck at it. She'd slugged down four or five drinks in a row, so that killed any chance of really talking.

"Why do I ride Uncle Bud?" she said. "Well, why does one ride a jackass? Because it's the shortest distance between two points. *Quad erat demonstandum*, which translated into canine means—"

"Look, Fay, this is important. If you think he can't pull this off, or that he might try to pull something on me—"

"Will you stop interrupting? It means never look for bones in a bottle. You remember that, Collie. It's the secret of my success."

"Good night." I got up and started for the garage. I was just about to the back door when she called, "Collie," and followed me out to the kitchen.

"I don't know, honey," she said, putting her arms around me. "There's something insidious about the guy. He sort of takes you over, and makes you over, and it's hard not to like him. But the things he's pulled on people . . . And as for this present deal—a man who would dream up a thing like this, Collie, he's considerably less than upright. If it would make him anything, and if he thought he could get away with it, he'd double-cross anyone."

"But you don't see how he could? You just razz him to see him squirm, like you do me?"

"Something like that. When a person can't stand herself, Collie, when she loathes herself . . ."

"It'll be all right," I said. "Everything will be all right afterwards."

"Will it? Do you really think any good can come from it?"

"It's got to, Fay. It's got to come from somewhere."

We stood there close together, her arms tightly around me. She squirmed contentedly, and her robe opened a little. She had nothing on underneath. Fay bent her knees a little, sliding her warm flesh against me. She took a long shivery breath. The sweet softness of her breasts seemed suddenly to harden. Then, she waited. All I had to do was make one little move. And somehow I couldn't make it. With any other dame, yes. But not with her. She meant too much to me. *This* had to mean more than it could now.

After a moment Fay looked up at me, eyes twinkling, a soft smile on her face. "Well, Collie, is this part of your college training? Not to take advantage of a lady in her cups?"

"I—I don't know," I felt rather embarrassed and foolish. "I mean, well, I never really went to college. Just some night classes when I didn't have to work."

"So?" She stood on tiptoe and kissed me, gave me a pat on the cheek. "Well, it's an excellent argument for the midnight oil."

"Look, I don't want you to think I wouldn't like to—"

"Also for abstinence. Go to bed, my friend. Yes, I really want you to. We have a nice thing here, and let us not louse it up."

She kissed me again, and gave me a push toward the door. I went to bed.

6

Usually, during the past fifteen-odd years, I'd hated to see morning come. That's a psychotic symptom, you know, not wanting to awaken—hating to face things that are bound to be more than you can handle. It had gotten so that I was almost always sick in the morning. I'd start vomiting almost as soon as I opened my eyes. I'd gone on that way for years, for more than fifteen years, and I guess I'd just about forgotten there was any other way. But *that* morning I knew better.

That morning—the morning after *that* night—it was like all those years had never been.

I waked up early, not long after daylight, and the way I was feeling you couldn't have paid me to stay in bed. I lay real still for a minute, sort of holding myself in, feeling the energy build up. Then, I jumped up, and for about the next ten minutes you'd have thought I *was* crazy. I "skipped rope." I shadowboxed. I did a handspring up onto the bed and off the other side, and I wound up by walking into the bathroom on my hands.

I was breathing a little hard, but that was all right. It was good to have done something to breathe hard about. I shaved and showered, using the toilet articles Uncle Bud had bought me. I got dressed, and went over to the house.

Fay was still asleep, of course. She hardly ever got up much before noon. I fixed myself a big breakfast, keeping quiet about it so as not to disturb her, and after I'd eaten I went back outside.

I sat out on the back porch a while, looking at the waist-high grass of the lawn. It looked to me like it was just kind of begging for it, just daring me to move in and cut it down to size. So finally I dug an old scythe up out of the garage and went to work on it.

Well, though, it wasn't much of a scythe, and that grass was almost as tough as wire. After an hour of hard swinging, I'd hardly made a dent in it.

I straightened up, and rested my back. I walked up to the far corner of the garage, and sized the yard up from that angle. It looked to me like I'd better do my cutting in rows, starting here on the outside and working in toward the house. I could keep track of the job better that way. I wouldn't actually cut any more, but at least it would show up better.

I started swinging again, cutting a broad swath clear down to where the trees began. I was standing there resting in the shade, when I saw a car coming. I ducked down out of sight, wondering who it was because I could tell it wasn't Uncle Bud. Then, the sun struck against the license plate, lighting up the lettering. And I jumped up and ran.

I ran straight down the lane toward it. It stopped, and I hesitated a moment, panting, and then I opened the door and climbed in.

Doc Goldman took out his pipe. He tamped tobacco into the bowl and struck a match to it. Not looking at me. Just looking straight ahead through the windshield.

"I'm sorry, Doc," I explained. "I couldn't stay there with you. You know I couldn't. It—it just wouldn't have been right! I'd have been worried about it."

"But this didn't worry you, simply walking out on a

friend? You thought that was all right?" He shook his head. "That's not very straight thinking, Collie. It's the kind of mixed-up, one-sided thinking that can get you into serious trouble."

"I'm not mixed up. It was just something that I had to do, so I did it."

"With a gallon of red wine, I suppose? And the rear end of a truck for transportation?" He laughed tiredly. "No, it wasn't too difficult tracing you, Collie. You're hardly what one would call nondescript. But with all that wine, I didn't expect you to get this far."

"That wasn't for me. It was a present. I bought it for the—for these people I'm working for."

"Here?" He motioned up the lane with his pipe. "Then, you lied to me when you said you didn't know anyone in this state?"

"No. I mean—well, I didn't really know them. I just met them that night, the night I met you. Kind of an elderly couple. We had a few drinks together, and—"

"Stop it, Collie! I've made a few discreet inquiries. I know who lives in this place."

I felt my face turning red. I wanted to tell him to go to hell; that it wasn't any of his business what I did. But he just wasn't the kind you could say things like that to. And I couldn't have done it anyway. He'd been too nice to me, and I knew he was trying to be my friend.

"She's a widow, isn't she, Collie?" he said. "She picked you up in a bar, just as, I suspect, any number of other women have—and for much the same reason. But being a nice guy, if a little naive, you didn't hang around. You knew it was the wrong thing to do, so you left. Then, yesterday, you changed your mind. You convinced yourself that wrong was right, so you came back and moved in."

"No! Not the way you mean it, Doc. I'm working here, really working. You can see that I am, and you can see there's plenty to be done." He glanced at the house and then skeptically at the patch of grass I had cut. "I'm not living with her," I explained hastily. "I've got a little apartment out there above the garage. Sure, I like her! I like her a lot, and she likes me. And she needs me. She—she drinks too much, and she needs someone to—"

"But, Collie! Collie, my friend." He laid a hand on my arm. "Don't you see— You *did* see the danger in such a situation a few days ago. You, by no means a well man, and a woman who also is not well, an alcoholic. The two of you together—a woman whose behavior is certain to be erratic and trying, at least at times, and a man who is apt to be upset by ordinary give-and-take."

"She needs me," I insisted. "Do you know what that means, to have someone really need you for the first time in your life?"

"I know. But, Collie, it still isn't right."

"It must be because when I woke up this morning, I was glad. I was glad to be alive, Doc, because I knew someone else would be glad. And people just aren't glad unless they need you. They may be nice and friendly, like you were, but if they don't need you, they can't really be glad. They can't really care whether you're alive or not. And when no one else cares, when it goes on that way year after year, Doc, and nobody cares . . ."

I stopped. I guess I'd said about everything there was to say. Doc cleared his throat uncomfortably.

"All right, Collie." He sighed. "I'll agree to your staying on here, but she'll have to be told about your condition." I gave him a scathing look and he added, "I can do it in a way so that she won't be alarmed."

"Not alarm her! You'll tell her that I'm on the loose from an insane asylum, that if I get crowded very hard I may haul off and start swinging. You'd tell her that—what the hell else could you tell her?—and you say she wouldn't be alarmed!"

"Now, Collie. I think I could pose the situation much better than that. Besides, it's for your own good, Collie. Yours and hers. I'd be violating my duty if I didn't do it."

The cords in my throat began to swell. I rubbed at my eyes, trying to brush away the red haze, and I said—I heard a voice saying, "Don't do it, Doc. If you do this to me, if you make me l-lose her, I'll—"

He turned full around in the seat. He put his hands up on the wheel where I could see them, watch them, and he simply sat there calmly. Looking into my face, and waiting.

The reddish haze went away. My throat relaxed. I leaned

back in the seat, feeling limp and empty and kind of dull. But knowing what to do. I opened the door of the car, and started to get out. He drew me back. Looked at me worriedly.

"Collie . . ." He hesitated. "If you'd just understand . . ."

"I understand. I'll get my coat and leave with you."

"No, wait a minute." He stared at me thoughtfully. "You *are* looking good, Collie. You look a hundred percent better than you did when you left my place."

"I feel better. At least I did, until you showed up."

He winced and went on studying me. It seemed like an hour before he spoke again. "Are you covering up anything, Collie? I was thinking that if Mrs. Anderson was the type who picked up men in bars, she'd quite likely have some pretty shady acquaintances."

"She's not that type. She did it with me, but that doesn't make her the type."

He nodded slowly. "Well, all right, my friend. For the time being, until you're a little better settled at least, I won't see her."

"Gosh, Doc. I—gosh, I just don't know how to thank you!"

"Don't," he said, sort of embarrassed. "I'm not entitled to any thanks."

We talked for a few minutes more. Finally, we shook hands and he left, backing down the lane to the highway instead of coming up into the yard.

I went back to the grass-cutting, but I didn't work at it long. I was too weak. That strain I'd been under when I'd thought he was going to see Fay had taken too much out of me.

I stretched out in the grass, letting the sun beat down into my face, hoping I'd never have to go through a thing like that again. Doc Goldman, I thought—my friend, Doc, one of the squarest guys that ever lived. And for the moment I'd been on the point of killing him. I shivered, feeling cold despite the sunlight. Doc—I'd almost killed Doc. And I probably would kill him if . . .

But that "if" was never going to be. Because he'd promised not to see her.

It didn't hit me till later that he hadn't promised not to call her on the telephone . . .

7

It was three nights later. We were all sitting around the living room table, Fay and Uncle Bud and I, studying the city map and going over Uncle Bud's notes. There were a lot of them, the notes, I mean. As Fay had said, he'd been planning this thing, working on it for months. And there wasn't much about Charles Vanderventer III that he didn't know. As a matter of fact, I guess he knew quite a bit more than the boy's own folks did. Because if they'd known what we knew, and if they'd done anything about it, there couldn't have been any kidnaping.

I got to thinking about that part afterwards, when all the hullabaloo broke loose. When there was a four-state alarm out and thousands of police were called up for extra duty, and hundreds of suspects were rounded up and questioned. Just guessing, I'd say that it must have cost someone several million dollars. And of course there's no way of counting what it must have cost the parents—what they went through.

And it was all so senseless, you know. It would all have been so easy to avoid.

The more I thought about it, the more it seemed to me that Bill Collins and Charles Vanderventer III were pretty much in the same boat. I know that sounds funny, but we were. Aside from Doc Goldman, who really wasn't able to do anything, no one was interested in either of us until the kidnaping. No one did anything to stop it. They must have known that he was practically a cinch for something like this, and they must have known that I—or someone like me—was a cinch for it. But no one did anything about us. They just let us rock along with a pat or a pinch now and then, but not really giving a damn about us, it seemed like, as long as we kept out of the way and were quiet.

But we were all in it then and plotting hard. I remember Uncle Bud pouring himself a drink and raising his eyebrows at me.

"Well, Kid. I guess those are our two best bets, either the playground or the picture show. You name it."

"Let's see," I said. "If it's the picture show, it would have to be tomorrow?"

"Well, we could wait another week. It would have to be on a Saturday. That's when they have the horse operas at this place, so that's when he always goes."

"And the nurse leaves him alone there sometimes while she and this chauffeur, Rogers, gad around?"

"She's done it, but not very much. We can't count on it. All we can count on is that she'll leave him alone while she goes to the women's rest room. A matter of fifteen or twenty minutes, maybe."

I hesitated. "She always stays that long?"

"I've timed her a dozen times, and it's never been less than that. Once it was a half an hour. She doesn't care for cowboy pictures, I guess, so she doesn't hurry."

"There's just one trouble with it. I couldn't already be in the show in the uniform. Fay would have to be inside. Then when the nurse left, she'd have to come out and tell me."

"I could do it." Fay shrugged. "And I'd just as soon do that as wait in the car."

"Yeah," I said, "but it kind of leaves a time gap in there. Something might happen between the time you came out and signaled me and I got into the show."

Fay gave Uncle Bud one of her mean grins. She'd been tapering down on the booze, doing a good job of it, and it was making her pretty sharp.

"Smart boy, isn't he?" she said. "Just when you think he couldn't see holes in Swiss cheese, he spots one like that."

"I said he was smart." Uncle Bud frowned at her. "I said so right from the beginning."

"So you did. Yes you did say that."

"Well . . ." Uncle Bud twisted in his chair, sort of turning his back on her. "I still think it might be the best of the two bets. The chauffeur's come into the show before and picked him up. After all, the kid's used to doing what he's told."

"He'll do what he's told just as well at the playground," I said, "and we won't have the nurse to worry about."

"But you'll have to ask for him at the playground. He'll be mixed in with a lot of other kids, you know, and you'll probably have to go to the playground matron. All that takes time."

"I guess I'll take it," I said. "That show's right down in the middle of town. If there was any trouble, we'd never be able to get away."

Fay laughed. She poured a little whiskey into her glass, and shoved the bottle toward me. "To Collie boy. May his sense of smell ever sharpen. Will you drink to that, Uncle Bud?"

Uncle Bud gave her a hard look; then, he laughed too, and said he'd drink to anything.

"But watch this stuff, huh?" he added. "I know you've been cutting down, but you can't be boozed up or have a hangover on this job."

Fay gave him another mean smile. Then, she smiled at me in a different way. And I knew she meant to be sober *before* we pulled the job.

"Okay, then, Kid." Uncle Bud turned back to me. "We'll make it at the playground on Monday. Tomorrow's out, because of the show, and Sunday he stays at home. So make it Monday."

"Around three o'clock," I said.

"Around three—a few minutes before to play it safe. The chauffeur, this Rogers, takes the boy to the playground at one; and he never picks him up before three-thirty or four."

We went on talking, running through the details again. After a while, I buttoned up the uniform jacket and put on the big outsize sunglasses, and let Uncle Bud look me over.

He'd bought the stuff in another city. It was all exactly like the real chauffeur's.

"Uh-huh." He nodded for me to sit down. "Once we do that touch-up job on your hair, you'll pass fine. You're maybe a little taller than the other guy, but no one'll be measuring you."

"These glasses kind of bother me," I said. "They make my face sweat, so that I can't see good."

"Well, you won't have to do much seeing with 'em. You won't put them on until the last minute."

I picked up my drink, and took a swallow. I couldn't think of anything more to say, but I kept feeling that I should.

"Yeah, Kid?" He was studying me. "Feeling a little nervous? Something on your mind?"

I said I wasn't particularly nervous. I wasn't worried about anything I had to do. "I'm just—uh—"

"He's wondering about the money." Fay winked at me. "He feels lost without his pockets full of money."

"Well, he won't feel lost much longer," Uncle Bud said. "We'll have it inside of a week, Kid. A hundred grand for me. A hundred and fifty for you and Fay to split. That's fair enough, isn't it?"

"It's fair. I guess that's what bothers me—thinking about all that money. I mean, I just can't believe that we're really going to get it."

"We'll get it," said Fay. "We'll get our share, or someone else will get something else."

Uncle Bud lighted a cigarette and jabbed the match down into an ashtray. He took a couple of short, quick puffs, his hand jerky when he raised the cigarette to his mouth. "This ain't something to horse around with. The Kid's got something on his mind, he'd better unload it."

I said it wasn't anything really, just an idea that had come to me. "I was just wondering if maybe there wasn't some way we could make a haul without actually going through with the kidnaping. Just start to, you know—kind of fake it—and then you step in and rescue the boy, something like that."

"Yeah?" He stared at me, sort of startled. "Yeah?" He poured himself a drink, keeping his eyes on the glass. "Go on, Kid."

"Well, the family would probably give you a pretty good reward, and you could probably get your job back in the department. There wouldn't be nearly as much money to divide, of course, but Fay and I could get by on a lot less."

"But how could you work it out, Kid? Where's your convincer? How do I play the big hero when no one gets caught?"

I scratched my head.

Fay laughed. "Down, boy. That's a good Collie."

"It can't be done, Kid." Uncle Bud shrugged. "There's just no way."

"No," I said. "I guess it can't be."

"Nope. Not a chance. So we'll just go right ahead Monday, and by this time next week we'll be sitting pretty . . ."

8

I had a funny dream that night, a damned bothersome one, I should say. One of those dreams in which everything turns out to be just the opposite of what you thought it was. It began back with that first day when I went into Bert's roadhouse, and this guy Bert—according to the dream—was really a pretty good guy. He hadn't wanted to act like he had; he'd done it because he was told to. He was just following orders—and I guess you know who was giving them—and it was the same way with Uncle Bud.

Uncle Bud hadn't planned the kidnaping. Fay had. She was calling the shots all the way down the line. The drinking was an act; she didn't drink nearly as much as she appeared to. That business about being half-helpless and needing someone to lean on was an act. She was tough, scheming, rotten all the way through—according to the dream. To get what she wanted, she'd slept with Uncle Bud and Bert; that was the way she held them in line. But they didn't mean anything to her, and I didn't. And when she was through with us we'd wind up with a lot less than nothing.

It was all jumbled and mixed up, of course, as dreams always are. But that's the way it ran generally. It seemed to go on for hours, but when I waked up sweating, groaning out loud, I saw that it couldn't have. The alarm clock said a little after midnight, and I hadn't gone to bed until almost eleven.

I sat up in bed and lighted a cigarette. The dream went away, the realness of it, and I stopped sweating and my pulse calmed down. I'd had these nightmares before. The psychiatrists had explained some of them to me, showed me that while they appeared to be different, they were all basically the same dream. Back in the beginning, I'd usually dreamed about getting beat up. I'd be in the ring with two or three guys, and they'd all have me out-classed. Or maybe there'd only be one, but the referee would be crooked. Or maybe the other fighter would be a woman or an old man with a beard—someone, you know, that I couldn't hit back at. Anyway, however it was, I'd get the hell knocked out of me.

That was about the worst thing that could happen to a

guy, you see. I mean, it had seemed like the worst thing
back in the beginning, when I wasn't much more than a
kid. As I got older, of course, I began to see that there could
be a lot worse things—like being sane—and not being able
to prove it. Or being crowded into a corner where you
might hurt someone. Or being around degenerates and
perverts so much that you got that way yourself. So I
dreamed about those things.

I'd always felt guilty about the Bearcat. Subconsciously,
although the feeling wasn't nearly as strong as it had been,
I'd felt that I ought to be punished. That was why I had the
dreams, and that was why I'd dreamed what I had about
Fay. Losing her, having things shape up so that I might lose
her, was the thing I dreaded most. It was the worst punish-
ment I could get, so in the dream I got it.

I lay awake a while, thinking the thing through, making
myself see how foolish it was. I was just drifting off to sleep
again, when a light flickered through my window. And I
jumped up and looked out.

It was a moonlit night. Far down the lane, I got a
glimpse of a car. I couldn't see anything else, any people in
or around it. Just a black car, parked with its lights off. I put
on my pants and shoes, slipped quietly out of the apartment and down through the trees.

The car pulled away, started backing off toward the highway just about the time I came even with it. But from the little I managed to hear and see, I knew I'd gotten myself out
of bed for nothing. It was just a man and a woman, a guy
and his girl friend. They'd driven in here to do a little pet-
ting, and now they were on their way again.

It was as innocent as that, but coming right on top of the
dream it bothered me a little bit. I couldn't help thinking
that it *could* have been someone else; someone *could* park
there and slip up to the house, and ten to one I wouldn't
know about it.

I went back to bed. After a long time, I went to sleep. But
even sleeping, I was still kind of bothered. I knew I
shouldn't be, that there was nothing to be bothered about.
But when a guy's whole life is wrapped up in just one thing
or just one person, well, he doesn't really need anything to
throw him.

Saturday, the next day, was kind of a bad day for me. Fay only took four or five drinks, but with the alcoholic fog pretty well gone from her mind she began to ask questions. She didn't appear suspicious, as though she thought I had something to hide. She simply wanted to know about me—as people do when they're deeply interested in a person. And I wanted her to feel that way. But you can see the spot I was in.

I couldn't tell her the truth. Even the half-way truth, glossing everything over, sounded like hell.

I'd been charged with murder after the fight with the Burlington Bearcat. Then, the charge had been reduced to second-degree manslaughter. I'd taken a plea to it, and the judge had made the sentence equal to the time I'd already spent in jail. I'd joined the army, and they'd bounced me out fast with a medical discharge. Since then, I'd gone from one institution to another, with a few cheap jobs in between. I didn't have the training for a good job. I couldn't give any references, and sooner or later my record always caught up with me.

That was the truth without going into a lot of details. What I told her was that I'd stopped fighting after I hurt a guy so bad that he never recovered from it. I said I'd been permanently banned from the ring after that, and anyway I didn't have the heart for it. But since I wasn't much good for anything else, I'd just sort of drifted.

That didn't satisfy her; I mean, she wanted to know more. But she saw I was getting upset, so finally she laid off. I went to bed early, completely worn out from the strain of all this. I slept well, and I waked up feeling pretty good.

I dressed and went over to the house. After breakfast, I went to work on the grass again. I'd just about shaken off the worrying. Like a guy will, I'd swung down through the bottom of the blues and come up on the other side. I wasn't entirely up, but I was coming up fast.

It was probably a couple hours after I went to work that I heard Fay stirring around in the kitchen. Then, maybe thirty minutes later, she came to the door and called to me.

I dropped the scythe and started across the yard. Wiping the sweat out of my eyes, mopping my face and arms with my handkerchief. I went up the steps and across the porch, opened the door, and went in. And—and then I just stood there, staring at her. Because I'd known she was beautiful, that she had the stuff to be, but I'd never thought Fay could be this beautiful. I didn't think that any woman could.

Her eyes were sparkling, crystal clear. Her hair had that soft, brushed-shiny look, and her face was rose-and-white softness that seemed to glow from the inside. She was wearing tan shorts, and a white off-the-shoulders blouse. She took a deep breath, smiling at me, and her breasts swelled. And I could see she was wearing nothing beneath the blouse.

"Well?" She tilted her head to one side, smiling. "How do I stack up as an advertisement for prohibition?"

"F-fine. You stack up period."

"Mmmm? Really think so? But you ought to make sure, shouldn't you?"

"Fay, Fay, honey—" I took a quick step forward, then I stopped, looking down at myself. "I guess with you so clean and pretty and everything, I ought to—"

I hesitated, kind of hoping she'd say it didn't matter. And I think she did start to say that. But this was something that meant a lot to her, as much probably as marriage would have meant, and in a sense it was marriage. It was something she wanted to be perfect, so, after a moment, she nodded.

"All right, Collie. It's a nice thing, as I recently remarked, so why louse it up?"

"I'll be right back," I said. "Just as soon as I wash up a bit."

"And you know where I'll be." She smiled. "I'll be ready. In fact, I think I may as well . . ."

Fay tugged suggestively at the blouse. Then she turned and went through the living room and into the bedroom.

I couldn't move for a second or two, and then I beat it out of there fast. I ran across the lawn, and up the stairs to my apartment. I turned the water on in the tub, and started shaving. I finished shaving, got in the tub, and scrubbed and soaked myself. Then, I put on all clean clothes and went back down the stairs again.

In all, I guess it had taken me about twenty-five minutes.

It couldn't have been any more than that. But in that little time—just that little time—everything changed for me.

I hadn't heard the car leave; I wouldn't have heard it with all the noise I was making in the tub. But it was gone and, of course, she was gone, too. I looked in the house, hoping against hope, hoping that it wasn't like I knew it was. But she was gone. Apparently, she'd gone dressed as she was, taking a coat with her maybe.

I sat down in the living room, and for a while I just sat, staring into space, staring at nothing, my mind a blank. Then, gradually I began to think again. And what I thought was that this was all so unnecessary, that it was one more piece of the pattern that had put me where I was.

Doc Goldman. Doc and the dozens of other doctors I'd come up against. They said that my thinking was one-sided, and, hell, compared with theirs, mine had more sides than a bar. They knew all about me—at least some of them did. But they knew me as something kind of isolated, something set off by itself and not really a part of the world. I was a case, not a person. What I thought or felt was of minor importance, if any. It was unreliable. I knew nothing, and they knew everything. And if I'd just hold still long enough, a year, two years, fifteen years, why, they'd fix me up in fine shape. Yes, sir, they'd take care of my case. Or if they didn't, it wouldn't matter. Because life would have passed me by.

I'd been listening to doctors for half my lifetime. But I couldn't remember one that had really listened to me, who'd actually given any thought to what I'd said. And why not? Tell me why not. I was the guy most concerned. I was the one guy who knew exactly what I was up against. I was the world's best authority on Kid Collins—not a case, but the *Kid himself*. I knew what he'd taken and how much he could take. And most of all, most important of all, I knew how people took him.

There wasn't any theory about it. There wasn't any of this business about how people ought to or should act. I *knew,* I'd learned by first-hand experience. and if anyone had listened to me, if Doc had listened . . .

Yeah, sure. I was in on a pretty rotten deal. But it had taken me more than fifteen years to get into it—more than fifteen years of holding still, of being the nothingness of a case. And . . . and Doc hadn't known about the deal. All he'd known was that I seemed to be getting along fine, that I had something to live for for almost the first time in my life. And still he hadn't listened to me. What I *knew* didn't matter, only what he *thought*.

I got the telephone directory, and looked up his number. I dialed it, and he answered immediately. I said, "Collie," and waited.

"Collie?" He hesitated. "Look, fellow, uh, where are you?"

"Right where I've always been."

"But—" He cleared his throat uncomfortably. "You remember, I didn't make any promises, Collie. I said we'd let it stand for the time being. And I only agreed not to see her. I didn't say that I wouldn't, uh, telephone."

"I know. You're a man of your word, Doc."

He was silent for a moment. When he spoke his voice sounded a little bewildered, kind of half-angry. "I didn't say a word that should have alarmed her, Collie. On the contrary, I was very careful to reassure her."

"Well, that makes her kind of crazy, doesn't it? She shouldn't have been alarmed, and she should have been reassured. But it turned out exactly the other way. She didn't react properly, did she, Doc? She's abnormal, isn't she?"

"Judging by her attitude, yes! She—"

"I know. I remember the time I had three spine taps in one month, and the time I had the electric-jolt treatment and the insulin-shock routine. There wasn't anything wrong with the treatment, you know. It wasn't the treatment's fault that I couldn't focus my eyes or stand up or remember my own name. That was mine; I just didn't react properly."

"Collie. Please listen to me."

"I remember a doctor at one of the places I was in, a guy that specialized in lobotomies. So he performed one of them right after another, and of course he was absolutely correct in doing it. But somehow the patients just wouldn't cooperate with him. They didn't react as they should have. He'd give 'em these swell prefrontals, just the prettiest jobs you ever saw. And these damned stubborn patients just wouldn't turn out right. I guess they probably liked being idiots, wouldn't you say? They liked being so stupid that they couldn't button their own pants or count the fingers on one hand. They liked—" I broke off, choking. "Let it go. Just let it go."

There was a pause and I could all but see him frowning. I could see the worry in his eyes. "I'm terribly sorry, Collie, but you must know that it was the only thing I could do. It's hardly my fault if Mrs. Anderson adopts an attitude that is completely unreasonable."

"That's the word all right, Doc. Now maybe you'll tell me what a reasonable attitude would be. She lives alone, remember, and her nerves are in pretty bad shape and she hasn't known me much more than a week. So tell me, Doc, just how should she have acted?"

"Well, I—I certainly don't think that she . . ." He paused. "Now, listen to me, Collie! I said I was sorry."

"You don't know, do you? You didn't know, but you know now. And you found out the easy way. Why didn't you do it to yourself, Doc? Why didn't you go to some of your normal people and tell 'em you were a mental case, and see how they acted?"

"Collie . . ." And now I could visualize the red flush on his face. "I did what I had to. I'm sorry that Mrs. Anderson took it as she did, and I'll be more than glad to— Is she with you, now?"

I laughed. I didn't say anything.

"You're at her house? Well, stay there and I'll come right out. I—you know I'm your friend, boy. I don't mean to throw anything up to you."

"I know. I'm glad I can remember."

"You'll stay there then—give me a chance to straighten this out?"

"I'm leaving here," I lied. "I'm hitting the trail again."

"No! No, Collie. If you don't feel that you can stay there, you must come back over here. We'll go ahead, just as we planned."

"I'm leaving, Doc. I'm hitting the trail, and don't try to pick that trail up. Because if you do . . . I might stop remembering."

I hung up the phone.

A minute later it started ringing again; it rang and rang, and then finally it stopped. And I went on sitting here, looking into nothingness. The tears streaming down my face.

I waited there at the house until around midnight. Then, I want out to the garage, stretched out on the bed and waited. At four in the morning, when I fell asleep, she still hadn't returned.

It was almost noon when I awakened and I was conscious of someone being in the room with me, I lay still, keeping my eyes slits, and looking out from beneath the lids.

It was Uncle Bud. He was seated near the bed, his hat pushed back on his smooth white hair. He was watching me, studying me rather. There was a thoughtful, calculating look on his too-friendly face; and I felt that I knew what he was thinking as well as he did.

So what if the Kid is a little off?—and it couldn't be more than a little. I can still use him. Use him, and then get rid of him . . . with Fay's help. Because the way she feels about the Kid, now, she'd be even more anxious to wash him up than I am.

I waked up; I opened my eyes, I mean. I looked surprised, and Uncle Bud apologized for walking in on me. He'd just that moment come in, he said, and I told him, sure, it was okay.

I went into the bathroom and washed. When I came out, he had that warm, warm smile turned on. The friendliness and sympathy stuck right out at me.

"You know what happened, Kid? Fay had a pretty big load on when she showed up at my place, and I'm not sure I got things straight."

"I know what happened. I checked with my friend the doctor."

"A hell of a note! Yes, sir, a hell of a note." He shook his head sadly. "Two people hitting it off like you were, and then a thing like this has to happen. But she'll snap out of it, Kid. Just give her a little time to get used to the notion, and she'll come around."

"Sure, she will. It won't bother her a bit."

"Well—" He glanced at me sharply. "Well, no, of course it won't. But we better not rush it, huh Kid? We better wait for her to lead. And, speaking of that, you just take it easy here and I'll bring you some breakfast."

Uncle Bud went over to the house and fixed me a tray, bacon and eggs and a big pot of coffee. Fay was really knocked out, he said, so sick and hungover she could hardly stand up. And that kind of put us on the spot, didn't it? It really fouled up the ball game, didn't it, Kid?

"It sure does. If we're going to pull it today, we ought to be leaving in a couple hours."

"Or less, Kid. Or less. I'd say to wait until tomorrow, but how do we know she'll be straightened out by then? Once she starts batting that jug, she's liable to be on it for a week."

"Yeah, that's right."

"Kid . . ." He hesitated. "What do you think, anyway? I'd take her place, go with you myself to take care of the boy. But I'm pretty well known in this town, and if someone should see us together . . ."

"Yes?" I said.

"Well, I don't think it would be a good idea. Maybe it wouldn't hurt anything, and maybe it would. The way I look at it, there's just no sense in taking chances."

I filled my coffee cup and lighted a cigarette. He waited, kind of fidgeting, wanting me to grab the ball and carry it. And I let him go right on waiting. I had to be absolutely sure, you see. It had to be his proposition.

"Well," he said, at last. "What d'ya say, Kid? What do you think? Me, now, I think you can swing it fine. You can do it just as well by yourself, as you could with Fay."

I took a swallow of coffee, hesitating; pretending to think it over. I screwed up my face thoughtfully, and slowly drained the cup. He watched every move. He leaned back in his chair, one arm thrown over the back, trying to appear easy and unanxious, but feeling so much the other way he just couldn't put it across.

Fay had called the turn on him all right. He was stupid—stupid and cheap. A little squeezing, and it cropped out all over him. It oozed out of him like sweat.

"Well," I said. "I'm pretty dumb myself. But if you think—"

"Yeah? Yeah, Kid?"

"If you think it'll be all right, why, okay."

"Swell! That's swell!" He jumped up beaming. "Now, if you're all through there, we'd better start getting you ready."

My hair is blond, almost yellow. Maybe I told you that? Well, anyway, it is—it—was—and the real chauffeur's hair was black. So that was where the dye touch-up came in.

I shaved, shaving extra close. When I was through, Uncle Bud took the razor and shaved my neck. He stood back and looked me over. He went over my face again, taking care of any little places I'd missed, and then he went to work with the dye.

I looked pretty funny when I was through—the sides and back of my hair black and the top of it yellow. The outsize sunglasses covered my lashes and brows, so we let them go. I put on the uniform, everything including the cap, glasses and gloves. Then, after Uncle Bud had checked me over, I stripped off the cap, jacket, glasses and gloves, and put on my hat. I was wearing a sports shirt. In the car, I'd look just about like any other guy out for a ride.

Uncle Bud helped me carry the uniform stuff downstairs. We put it down on the floor of the station wagon, behind the front seat, and I got in. Uncle Bud wished me luck. He beamed at me—almost laughing, he was so happy. And I almost laughed myself. I drove off, wondering why it was always the stupid people who figured everyone else to be stupid. Why they always think they can outsmart the other guy. Because I wasn't supposed to be bright, of course, but even an idiot could have seen through this stunt.

I'd never meant anything to him. Now that I didn't mean anything to Fay either, and since I'd practically told him how he could cash in and play it absolutely safe . . . Well, you see what he was going to do. What *they* were going to do.

And it looked like a very sweet set-up for them.

Everything seemed to fit together perfectly. They could even use Doc Goldman to back up their story.

Fay had felt sorry for me, and given me a job. Then, when Doc had told her about my background, she'd fired me—giving me until the following day, Monday, to clear out. She'd slept late that day, *this* day, and when she waked up she found that I'd stolen her car. She hadn't known quite what to do—being so innocent and unworldly, you know. So she'd called Uncle Bud, and he remembered I'd done some talking about the Vanderventer boy. He hadn't thought anything of it at the time, just supposed it was some wild talk. But if I was an escaped lunatic and a car thief . . .

Well, maybe I didn't have it figured exactly right. But it was close enough. I was due to get killed. Uncle Bud was due—or thought he was—to be a hero.

Knowing what I did, I couldn't say why I was going ahead. Somehow, I didn't really think about the why of it. It just seemed like something I had to do—like I'd been set in a rut and had to follow it out to the end. I was hurt, of course; hurt and sore at the whole world. And probably that was why. But I don't know. All I knew was that I had to go ahead, and that I needed an angle to do it. Something that would pull them into the deal, and hold them in it.

It would drive them nuts, I thought. They figured on cashing in fast and easy, and it wasn't going to be that way. I'd make them go ahead. They'd have to play it right out to the end . . . with an escaped lunatic for a partner. A lunatic who was suspicious of them, who knew they'd tried to kill him. And before it was all over, they'd probably be ten times crazier than they thought I was.

But I needed an angle. I had to have an angle.

That neighborhood was the finest in the city, just about the fanciest I'd ever seen anywhere. There were a few apartment houses, with pools and fountains in front and long wide walks leading up to them. But almost everything was estates. The houses sat far back from the street, so far and so hidden by trees that they could hardly be seen. Most of them, most of their yards rather, were enclosed by walls that cut them off from the street. I was parked at the corner of one of these walled places.

The playground was just across the street ahead of me. It covered a square block, and it had about everything you could name in the way of play equipment. Practically all of the kids that came here, of course, had as much or more at home. But this private park gave them something they didn't have at home—something that ordinary kids take for granted; a chance to play with other children. So I guess their folks felt it was necessary.

The grounds were enclosed by a high spiked-steel fence, with a gate on each side. Across one end, fronting on this street and a side street, was a brick clubhouse. I suppose you'd call it that. Anyway, it was a place where the kids could romp in bad weather, and with rest rooms and so on.

The gates weren't guarded; I guess a guard for each one would have been pretty expensive. They weren't locked either, since the matron had twenty-five or thirty kids on her hands and she couldn't keep running back and forth to the gates.

She was a fairly young woman, dressed all in white like a nurse. She was kind of pretty, too, and also rather flustered—and—cross-looking. Because children like those, she could only crack down on them so hard. She could tell them what to do, but she couldn't really insist or get tough with them, if she wanted to keep her job. And it looked like she wasn't the only one who knew it. She'd been chasing after them, straightening out first one then the other, ever since I'd driven up. Now, finally, she had them all together in the middle of the playground, trying to get some kind of ring-around-a-rosy game started.

I took off my sunglasses and wiped them. I looked at the dashboard clock. It was five minutes after three. If he kept to his usual schedule, the real chauffeur would be showing up between three-thirty and four. So I had to be moving—if I was going to move. I had to, but I couldn't. I hadn't spotted my angle yet.

I put the glasses on again and looked back over at the

playground. I looked just in time to see a kid, a little boy, give a girl a shove. She sat down hard on her bottom, squalling like she'd been killed. The matron shook her finger at the boy and squatted down in front of the little girl. She dusted her off and petted her, put her on her feet again. She straightened up and looked around for the boy. Then she sort of shrugged, and went back to the game. Maybe she thought he was still in the group, because with all those kids it would be easy to overlook one. Or maybe she thought he'd gone to the toilet. Anyway, she couldn't be bothered. And I mean she really couldn't be. She had maybe thirty kids to look after, so she couldn't devote her whole time to one of them.

But I could. Any guy who wanted to pick one off could do it. So I knew where the little boy was.

He'd gone off to the clubhouse, but he hadn't gone inside. Instead, he'd scooted through the patio, dropped down on his hands and knees on the other side, and started crawling along the row of sandboxes. He was headed straight for the gate. From the way he went about it, you could tell he'd done it plenty of times before.

I started the car, watching him as he reached out from behind a sandbox and eased the gate open a few inches. His hair was the same color as the Vanderventer boy's. They were about the same size, too, but I could see he was older. He must be at least nine, I guessed, and probably he was as old as ten.

He was my angle. He could be the angle—*if* he got out.

And he did.

He did it so fast that I almost missed it. One second he was snaked down behind the sandbox. The next second he was out the gate, running stooped along the concrete base of the fence. At the rear of the clubhouse, he straightened up casually and walked on down to about the middle of it. Then, he took a cigarette from the pocket of his little sawed-off pants and tapped it against his wrist a few times.

He took a lighter from another pocket, and lit it. He leaned against the building, one foot crossed over the other, puffing away like a little old man. I put the car into gear. I drove past the playground, the fenced part, and stopped at the rear of the clubhouse.

He flicked his fingers at me in a kind of wise-guy salute. "Hi, Rogers," he said, sauntering forward. "What do you know, for sure?"

I mumbled something, hello, or how are you, or something like that. Or maybe I didn't either. Because I was pretty mixed up to begin with, and the way he talked and acted, it didn't do anything to straighten me out.

"Okay?" He hesitated with his hand on the fender. Then he nodded at me through the windshield, went to the door, and climbed in. "How about a little ride, Rog? I want to talk to you about Charlie, and this will be my last chance."

I got the car started again. I started it with a jerk. He was doing exactly what I wanted him to do, doing everything for me. But, well, I just don't know. I just couldn't think.

"Don't remember me, do you, Rog?" He leaned back, propping his feet up on the dashboard. "Well, I guess you wouldn't. I've been on the Coast for six months—just here for a few days with Grandma—and I have to go back to Paris tonight. That's the way the judge made it when my parents got divorced. Six months with Dad in the States and six months with Mom."

He lighted another cigarette, and held the package out to me. I shook my head, looking into the rear view mirror. There was a car or two behind me, but neither was Uncle Bud's. I wondered if I'd figured him and Fay wrong.

"Now, about Charlie," the boy said. "What's happened to him, anyway Rog? What kind of shoving around are those goofy parents of his giving him?"

"Shoving around?" I mumbled. "I, uh, I guess I don't know what you mean."

"Never mind. I know how they treat him, how they've always treated him. He's been sick for years, and he's getting sicker. And the worse he gets the tougher they make it for a him. Making a man out of him, they call it. Teaching him responsibility . . . Boy, I wish I was a little bigger! I'd get me a club, and . . ."

I saw them now, Fay and Uncle Bud. They were in his car. Fay was driving and they were coming up fast.

"Something wrong, Rogers?" The boy gave me a knowing look. "Want me to duck out of sight?"

"Just some friends of mine," I said. "And, no, I want you to sit right up. Just act like—"

"I get you. You were too early to pick Charlie up, so you're killing a little time with a pal."

I swung into the curb and stopped. Their car shot past us, skidded to a stop, and Uncle Bud jumped out. He started toward us at a run, his hand inside his coat. Then, he got a good look at the boy, and his mouth dropped open. And he stopped as suddenly as the car had.

I got out. I sauntered up to him, deliberately looking puzzled. "What's the matter?" I asked. "What are you two doing out this way?"

"I—we—" He shook his head helplessly, his eyes wavering. He'd planned on doing just one thing, and now he didn't know what the hell to do. "That b-boy," he said, at last. "Damn it all, Kid, you got the wrong boy!"

"Huh!" I let out a grunt. "But he looks—"

"Well, damn it to hell, he's not! A blind man could see he's not."

"I told you. I told you I couldn't see good with these glasses. But there's no use in getting sore. I'll just take him back and get the right one tomorrow."

"Just like that, huh? Hell, of all the dumb—"

"He won't say anything. I'll make him think it's some kind of game."

"Yeah, but—" Uncle Bud hesitated. "But it's so damned late! You're practically a cinch to run into the other chauffer."

"I can make it," I explained, "and I'm sure the kid won't talk. He'll be afraid to, see? He slipped off from the playground, and he'll be—"

"Okay! All right!" He made up his mind suddenly. "But get moving, will you? Snap into it, and I'll see you out at the house."

Uncle Bud ran back to his car, pushing Fay back in just as she started to get out. They drove off with him at the wheel, and I went back to the station wagon.

"Well, Rogers . . ." The boy nodded at the dashboard clock. "I've got to be getting back to the playground."

"Right away," I agreed. I pulled the car around in a fast U-turn. "Now, about this little ride of ours. I'll appreciate it if you don't say anything about it."

"I won't," he promised, "and don't you say anything either. Just give me a minute to duck into the clubhouse. Then you can pick up Charlie, and no one'll know a thing."

I turned at the corner of the playground and parked at the side of the clubhouse. He opened the door kind of reluctantly. Sat, hesitating, half-in and half-out of the car. Then, he turned slowly around and stared thoughtfully into my face. And for a moment he looked every bit as old as he talked.

"Charlie's sick," he said. "Awful sick. I can't do anything about it, and anyway I've got to go back to Paris tonight."

"I'll see about him," I said hurriedly. "I'll look after him. Don't you worry."

"You better. You sure as heck better . . . Rogers."

He slid out of the car, looked back in for a second. "Take it easy," he said. "His folks need a good jolt, but don't be too tough on 'em."

Then he was gone. So quickly that it was hard to believe that he had ever been there. I got out of the car right away, but by the time I reached the playground he was nowhere in sight.

I opened the gate. I went inside, leaving it off the latch. It was three-thirty—it *had been* three-thirty when I left the car. The real chauffeur was due at any time. But I had to go through with this deal, and it was now or never.

They were still out in the middle of the playground, the children and the matron. I stopped about twenty feet away, and after a moment she turned and saw me.

"Oh, hello, Rogers!" She said it in the half-haughty way people use when they think they're better than you are— and feel that they have to keep proving it. "You're early for a change, aren't you?"

I didn't say anything; just touched my fingers to my cap. She gave her head a little toss, and looked around at the children. "Charles, Charles Vanderventer," she called. "Oh, here you are! Run along with Rogers now."

He moved out of the group, a pale weak-looking kid. He looked at me uncertainly, and then he looked at her.

"Is that Rogers?" he said, puzzled.

"Is it— Oh, my goodness!" She took him by the

shoulders and gave him a push. "Who else would it be?"

He started toward me, moving slowly. Feeling, knowing, that something was wrong, but afraid to say so. He followed reluctantly as I turned around and started toward the gate. I walked fast for a few steps, listening to him, listening to his footsteps. He kept that same slow pace, so I had to slow down, too. I couldn't let him get too far behind, and I couldn't hurry him. He was used to doing what he was told, but I couldn't lean on that too hard. If I tried to rush him, if he got scared enough . . .

"Oh, Rogers!" It was the matron. "Rogers!"

I paused, turned partly around.

"Charles has had a pretty trying day. Will you tell—will you please tell Mrs. Vanderventer that I suggest he stay at home tomorrow?"

I waved my hand. I started toward the gate again, and after a long moment I heard the boy following. Moving as slowly as he could. Barely dragging his feet.

My glasses were steaming over. I shifted them and they cleared for a moment, and then they seemed to fog up worse than ever. The gate was less than thirty feet away, but I could hardly see it. I glanced over my shoulder, and I could barely see the boy. Everything was blurred, a watery, hazy blur. Everything was kind of meaningless. I was a blind man, a man who had blinded himself to get something. And, now, whatever it was I'd wanted, was slipping away from me.

All it once my mind was a complete blank. I didn't know where I was. I didn't know how I had gotten here, or what I was doing or supposed to be doing. I was just there, here, walking across a children's playground. A guy in hot, funny-looking clothes, with a little boy tagging along behind him.

And how, why, what it was all about, I didn't know. I guessed it must be some kind of a gag. The only thing I could think of was that I'd blanked out there in Bert's roadhouse, and they'd dressed me up in these clothes and dumped me out here. It could have happened. I'd pulled blanks before when my mind got too tight, and people had done some funny things to me when I had.

I sort of laughed to myself, going along with the gag,

thinking the joke would be on them when that crazy Jack Billingsley showed up. We'd been heading for the coast, see, me and that crazy Jack Billingsley. So the car had broken down, and I'd started back to the garage to get help, and somehow Jack had got it running again and . . .

I stumbled. I almost fell flat on my face. I yanked the glasses off and wiped them—cleaned them off good. And the bright sunlight struck into my eyes. And suddenly I knew where I was and why, and what I had to do.

I slapped the glasses back on. I whirled around, grabbed the boy by the hand and yanked him along with me. It was only a few steps to the gate, but there couldn't be any more of the foot-dragging. My nerves wouldn't take it. There wasn't time.

The boy whimpered a little when I grabbed him. Now he was hanging back, trying to, and I was afraid he might get up the nerve to yell. So I stooped and picked him up in my arms. That quieted him; paralyzed him with fear, I guess. I straightened up, and started through the gate.

And a big black limousine pulled in at the curb, and a chauffeur hopped out. He was dressed exactly as I was. He was the man I was supposed to be.

He dusted at his trousers, like a man will when he first gets out of a car. He took his sunglasses off and wiped them, gave me a glance and a nod, and put them back on again.

I nodded back at him. I went through the gate and down the steps to the walk. He started toward me, still dusting at himself. We passed each other. He went up the steps and through the gate. I started down the walk.

I reached the corner of the clubhouse. I stepped behind it, glancing over my shoulder, the real chauffeur had stopped and was staring at me.

I don't know how it came about. Whether he got a glimpse of the boy's face, or whether it had just taken that long for the situation to sink in on him. Probably it was the last. A thing can be so completely startling that it doesn't startle.

Anyway, the man swung into action fast. He didn't even yell, which, of course, he should have. He came charging through the gate in a leap, and down the steps in another. And he came pounding up the walk after me, fists churning, his head ducked. All action and nothing else.

I backed away from him, getting further behind the clubhouse, still holding onto the boy. When he was right on top of me, I stuck my fist out. I gave him a straight arm with a fist at the end of it, and he piled right into it with his face.

His glasses exploded. I felt his nose flatten and crunch. He reeled, wobbled on his heels, and toppled forward. He was out like a light, hit harder than I could have hit him. And no one had seen it. That fancy clubhouse was in the way, and the estate walls were in the way. They were walled off from the world, and the world was walled off from them.

I ducked around the corner. I put the boy flat on the floor of the car, climbing in over him, keeping a foot on him while I shucked out of the uniform stuff and put on the hat. Then, I wheeled the car around in a U-turn, crossed through the intersection, and headed for the highway.

The Vanderventer chauffeur was still lying where I had left him. As I turned the comer and the playground vanished from view, he was still sprawled behind the clubhouse. There'd been no cars passing by at the moment I gave it to him. But several had passed since then, and others were passing now. Yet no one stopped. They had other things to do, and it was none of their business if a man had fallen down.

I'd gone a couple of miles before I realized I had my foot on the boy. I lifted it off fast, and gave him a little pat. There was nothing to be afraid of, I told him. He'd just stay there and take it easy, and no one would hurt him.

He looked up at me, his big blue eyes filled with tears, his lips trembling and as pale as his face.

"All right. All—" He gulped. "I'll—I'll—"

He tried to tell me that he'd do what I'd said, but it got all tangled up in a sob. I told him not to try.

"Just rest, Charlie boy. Just be real nice and quiet, and

everything will be fine. I won't hurt you. I won't let anyone else hurt you."

I went on talking to him, soothing him. I guess he must have believed what I said, because the sobbing stopped and a little color came back into his face.

I turned on the car radio, keeping the volume low.

There was nothing on the air yet about the kidnaping, I didn't think there would be, but I was curious to know when the news would break. How long it would take. Apparently the chauffeur was still knocked out, lying where I had left him. And no one had stopped to see why he was there. The matron? Well, I was kind of puzzled about her, too. Because she must have seen the two of us together, and she must have known that things weren't as they should be. But—well, there you were. That's the way it usually goes. People who might do something that needs doing are too busy to do it. The others don't give a damn.

Yes, the police department was on the job. Relatively speaking, that was just about the best patrolled area in the city. In this section there were regularly assigned squad cars covering a five-mile area. The way it worked out on paper, the cars were supposed to cover as much territory as a dozen men on foot. And they *could,* too—they could "cover" it all right. But the police in it couldn't do a hell of a lot more than that. They couldn't drive lickety-split all day and see everything they should see. The officers couldn't be looking into trouble while they were driving around. If there was trouble, they had to leave the car—and the radio—while they investigated. And if something popped, meanwhile, it had to wait until they got back.

That was the set-up. The same kind of "efficiency" arrangement you find in lots of cities. It saved money for the taxpayers, and it was good business—"running the department on a business-like basis." At least, it must have seemed that way then.

Ordinarily, it should have taken about half to three-quarters of an hour for the trip from the playground to the house, but I took the trouble to drive slowly so as not to attract attention from the police or anybody. It was a strain doing that, talking to the boy now and then, and listening to the radio, so I turned it off. I wanted more and more to open up the station wagon and get there as fast as I could, but I kept well within the speed limits. Then somehow—maybe because I was trying so hard—I managed to get lost. It was well over an hour and a half before I pulled up in the yard of the house.

Uncle Bud and Fay were at the kitchen door. Just standing there, white-faced and kind of dazed-looking, almost motionless. Inside the house, I could hear the radio blaring the news of the kidnaping. So it was out now. I took my time walking up to them, then I stopped just off the steps and listened.

Like all firsthand reports, it was confused. The facts of the kidnaping were more or less there, but the story was all garbled. They had no description of me, nothing beside the fact that I was "fairly tall and of medium build." They didn't know what kind of car I'd used.

Both the matron and the chauffeur were being questioned. All available police, including those off-duty, had been ordered to the area. The entire neighborhood had been blocked off, a search of every estate in the vicinity was underway, all servants—particularly uniformed-chauffeurs—were being "intensively grilled."

The boy's parents were "prostrated." The mayor had demanded "all-out action," the police commissioner was "pressing for an immediate solution of the case," and the chief of police had promised that "no stone would be left unturned."

The news had just broken, but everyone that was anyone was all ready with a statement. They were so ready with their predictions and promises and demands, you might have thought they'd been expecting something like this. But I don't guess they had, or if they had it hadn't bothered 'em much.

I went back to the car and around to the other door. I spoke to the boy, and then I lifted him out gently and started up the wall. He was sound asleep, exhausted with the excitement and strain. I was practically knocked out myself, but naturally everything had hit him a bit harder.

Fay and Uncle Bud moved out of the doorway; I'd have knocked them out of it if they hadn't moved. I brushed past them, carried the boy into the spare bedroom, and laid him down on the bed. I slipped off his shoes, partly unbuttoned his shirt. Then, I went back into the living room, pulling the door shut behind me.

Fay and Uncle Bud had snapped out of it a little. Enough, at least, to wobble back into the living room and fix themselves a drink. I fixed myself one, and sat down. Fay looked at me out of the corner of her eyes. She gave me a straighter look, her lips trembling as she tried to smile. I stared back at her, and she dropped her eyes and the smile went away.

Then it was Uncle Bud's turn. I went through the same thing with him. Staring through him, forcing the smile back into his face, making him look away. They both sat looking at the floor—almost holding their breaths, sort of poised on the edge of their chairs. They looked like they'd jump if I said boo, and I left them that way. It was the way I wanted them to feel.

I leaned back and sipped at my drink, listening to the radio. There was nothing new. Just the same hot air without anything behind it. I got up and fixed another drink. I switched the radio off, and sat back down.

"Well, what's the matter? I didn't surprise you, did I?"

Fay's head came up. Her breath went out in a deep, quavery sigh. "*Surprise* us!" she said. "Surprise us! Oh, Collie, how—why in the world did you do it?"

"Why not? It was what we planned on. It was what I was supposed to do."

"B-but—but not that way! Not after you'd made a mistake, and it was so late you were almost sure to-to-to—" Her voice broke, and she covered her face with her hands.

She rocked back and forth, kind of sobbing and laughing, smiling and frowning, all at the same time.

That seemed to bring Uncle Bud back to life. He let out a laugh, slapping his hand on his knee.

"Surprise?" He beamed at me. "And what a surprise, Kid! I got to hand it to you, boy. I bet there ain't another man in the country that could have pulled a stunt like that and got away with it!"

"There's plenty that could do it. All you'd have to do is get them sore. Pick yourself a guy that's a little bit off and then try to throw a curve under him, and he'd do it."

"Yeah?" He weaved around that one. "Well, I know what

you mean, Kid. You hold the short end of the stick just so long, and then you start swinging it. You've had enough, see? People just don't want to get along with you, no matter how willing you are, so finally—"

"Shut up!"

"Huh? Now, look, Kid—"

"I said to shut up!"

"But—" He brushed the back of his hand against his mouth. "W-well, sure. Anything you say, Kid."

"You gave me a card when I first came here," I said. "You wrote your name and your address and telephone number on it in case I had to get in touch with you. It's in your own handwriting, remember. Not just a printed business card that I might have come by accidentally."

I paused, letting it sink in on him. He wet his lips uneasily.

"You wouldn't have found that card on me today," I went on. "You couldn't have got it back. I won't tell you where it is, but I'll tell you this: I've got a good friend or two around the country. Even a guy like me will pick up a few friends. And if anything should happen to me, the cops will get that card mighty fast and they'll be told where it came from."

I was lying, of course. Probably Uncle Bud had a good hunch that I was. But he wasn't very bright, and he didn't have much in the way of guts. And if his hunch was wrong, if I *wasn't* lying . . .

His eyes flickered as he tried to make up his mind. He brushed at his coat nervously, his fingers lingering at the ominous bulge under his handkerchief pocket. He wanted to do it; he wanted to so bad that he could taste it. But he couldn't quite talk himself into the job. It was a pretty screwy thing I'd told him; like something out of a cheap movie. But—well, I was a pretty screwy guy, wasn't I? I'd already outsmarted him once today, and with a stunt that made less than no sense at all. So if I'd done it once, why wouldn't I do it again? How the hell did he know what I might do?

"Collie," said Fay, breaking the silence. "What—what is *this?* What are you getting at?"

I didn't answer her, or even look at her. I sat watching Uncle Bud a moment longer, grinning at him. Then, I got up and walked over in front of him.

"Well, how about it? You've got a gun. You were all set to use it an hour or so ago. Why don't you do it, now?"

His mouth opened. His lips moved silently, helplessly. I caught him by the shirt front, and yanked him to his feet.

"Can't make up your mind, huh? You're scared, stupid and scared. Well, I'll give you a little help. Maybe if you get good and sore . . ."

I gave him a little jolt under the heart. Just a little tap with my fist. Uncle Bud grunted, his face went white, and I tapped him again. Around the heart, down in the kidneys, and up on the wishbone. I held him with one hand and fed him those little jolts with the other. And his face seem to turn from white to green, and his tongue slid out from his teeth.

I reached under his coat grabbed his gun, and shoved it into my belt. Then, I dropped him down into his chair, and went back to the sofa.

Uncle Bud sat bent over, hugging himself. He wasn't really hurt bad, just temporarily paralyzed with pain. But I guess he thought he'd been about half-killed.

Fay frowned at me. Scared, but more puzzled it seemed than anything else. "Collie!" she said sharply. "I want to know what this is all about!"

"You know, Fay. I told you right from the beginning. I told you I wasn't stupid, and I didn't like for people to treat me like I was."

"But, but what's that got to do with it?" She paused and went on in a lower voice. "Is it—does it have something to do with yesterday? I'm terribly sorry about that, darling. It just came as such a shock to me that I couldn't think; I didn't know what I was doing for a while. Then I ran off and started drinking and made such a mess of myself that I was ashamed to face you."

"Forget it. I know how you felt and what you felt. So don't bother to tell me."

"But . . ." She hesitated again. "Is it—I'm sorry I let you down today, Collie. But I just didn't see how I could go through with it. I wouldn't have been any good to you. The way I felt, I'd have been almost sure to spoil things."

"But you pulled yourself together. You felt well enough to

leave right behind me. To be Johnny-on-the-spot after I'd pulled the job."

"Well." She nodded slowly. "Yes. Uncle Bud thought we ought to do that much to help, at least. If something went wrong—if there was trouble, we might be able to pull you out of it. I was still sick, but I was worried about leaving you to do everything. And Uncle Bud thought I—we—"

"That's right, Kid." It was Uncle Bud getting back to normal. "That's just the way it was. We were concerned for you, having to do everything yourself, and we figured we'd better kind of keep an eye on things."

I laughed. I didn't say anything, just laughed the one time and chopped it off short.

Fay's eyes flashed. "And it's a good thing we were there! If we hadn't been, you'd have taken the wrong boy."

"Yeah? It hasn't maybe occurred to you that I picked that boy up deliberately?"

"Deliberately! But, but why would you do that? What— now, look!" she said. "I'm getting fed up! What's he talking about, Uncle Bud?"

He looked at me uneasily. He cleared his throat, tried to work up a smile, and it looked like something on a corpse. Fay frowned. She asked him again what I was talking about.

It was a pretty good act. You'd have almost thought she didn't know.

"Answer me!" she said. "I swear, if this keeps up much longer, I'll, I'll—!"

"Now, now." He squirmed. "There ain't nothing to get excited about. The Kid's just kinda got the wrong slant on things, an'—and I don't blame him, y'understand. I don't hold the slightest grudge whatsoever. He's been under a big strain today."

'Will you stop stalling and tell me!" said Fay loudly.

"Well, uh, you remember what we were talking about the other night? About maybe not actually going through with the snatch—just faking it kind of, and then having me step in and collect a fat reward?"

Fay nodded. "But we couldn't do it. There was just no way we could. So what about that?"

"Well, uh, yeah, there was a way all right. Just one way to

make it look good. And I guess that's kind of what the Kid's thinking about. Then maybe the thought I was jealous of you two or something. Of course, he's all wrong, but—but you see how it might look to him. You act like you're completely washed up with him. The Kid figures we're both plenty leery of having him around. So when he had to go by himself today, and then we show up, why—"

Fay's glass slid out of her hands. It bounced against the carpet, and then toppled onto its side; rocked back and forth, the ice tinkling.

She stooped and picked it up. She reached out and set the glass on the table. She wasn't looking at what she was doing—she was staring at me—and it fell to the floor again. Fay didn't seem to notice. There was an expression on her face I'd never seen before. A kind of waking-up expression. It was the way a blind person might look if he was suddenly able to see. If he really saw himself for the first time in his life.

"So that's what you think," she said. "That's what you think of me."

"Why not?" I said.

"Yes. Why not? If a person won't stop at kidnaping, why would he stop at murder? I don't think it makes much difference about yesterday, Collie. About what happened or didn't happen. It may have brought about this situation a little sooner, but with people like us—people who've become what we have—we were bound to arrive at it." She rubbed her eyes tiredly, and shook her head. "You were wrong about not being stupid, Collie. You are. I am. Uncle Bud also, to cite a self-evident fact."

"Now, now," said Uncle Bud. "What's the sense in all this glooming around? We had a little misunderstanding, but it's all over now. We're all square with the world again. We got what we wanted, and now we're all set to collect."

Fay laughed. "Collect. Yes, gentlemen and lady, now we can collect."

"I said so, didn't I?" Uncle Bud turned to me. "Now, I've been thinking, Kid. There's nothing in the news about the station wagon, but isn't there a chance that that first boy might peep? I know it don't look like he would. He wouldn't want to admit he'd sneaked off and gone for a ride with a stranger. And probably if he did admit it, that matron would swear he was lying. But the cops won't be passing up any bets on this one, so . . ."

Fay got up suddenly and went into her bedroom. I started to get up, too just instinctively without thinking. Wanting to go after her, to ask her if something was wrong. And then I caught myself, and I settled back down again.

"I can ditch it over at my place, Kid. What do you think?"

"What? Oh, well, yeah. Maybe you'd better do that. I'm pretty sure the boy won't say anything, but someone else might have spotted it."

"Right. I'll take it with me then when I go and leave you my car. I can pick up another heap to get around in until we pull down our jackpot. Now—" He reached for the bottle, and poured his glass half-full. He was trying to be friendly and casual, but his hand shook. Underneath his big, easy smile, he was scared stiff. "Now, I figured I'd mail the ransom note tonight, if that's okay with you. They'll get it the first thing in the morning."

"Look," I said. "We've been all through this. You know what you have to do, and there's no point in asking me about it."

"Yeah, but . . ." He hesitated. "Well, I don't want you to get any more wrong ideas, Kid. I don't want to do anything that maybe you, uh—"

"I won't get any ideas without a damned good reason. Just don't give me any reason, and I won't get any ideas."

His smile warmed up, began to look a little more natural. "Now, you're talking, Kid. Hell, there's no use getting all up in the air and acting unfriendly, is there? We had a little misunderstanding—and I don't blame you a bit, see?—but now that we got it cleared up—"

"All right. Let's just cut it off there. I'm tired of kicking it around, and I'm tired period."

"Sure. Sure, Kid," he said hastily. "Now, what do you think about—?" He broke off, started another sentence. "I think I'd better have something of the boy's, Kid. A label out of his clothes, or maybe his handkerchief. Something to send with the ransom note, so they'll know it's just not some crank writing. A case like this, you know, there'll—"

I got up, cutting him off, and went into the bedroom. I

eased the boy's handkerchief out of his pocket, saw that it was initialed, and took it back into the living room. Uncle Bud said it would do fine; it was just what he needed. And maybe he'd better be running along now.

I walked out to his car with him. He gave me the keys to it and got into the station wagon. But he still didn't leave. He kept rambling on, thinking of things to say.

"That uniform and stuff, Kid. Better get rid of it right away. Take it out and—"

"And bury it. I know. I'm going to."

"Better get to work on that hair right away, too. Scrub it out until there ain't a trace of the dye left in it."

I said I would. I knew everything I had to do, and I'd do it. But he still didn't leave. He still sat there, fidgeting with the car keys, making conversation. So, finally, I did the only thing I could do. He'd made a half a dozen starts at doing it, but he was afraid to carry through. So I took the lead. I shook hands with him.

And a minute or so later he drove off.

I buried the uniform and the things that went with it. I came back up from the trees, returned the spade to the garage and went up to the apartment. I washed my hair out, flopping down on the bed for a while afterwards. But tired as I was I couldn't rest. I kept tossing around, trying to straighten my mind out. And I sure didn't feel much like laughing, but somehow I wanted to laugh.

Because I'd played one hell of a joke on myself.

Doc Goldman had called the turn on me, all right. My judgment was anything but good. Guys with my background—and maybe a lot of guys without it—can't think very far ahead. They knock themselves out getting something. They just have to have it, it seems like. And then it turns out to be something they don't want, and they don't know how to get rid of it.

I'd looked forward to making Fay and Uncle Bud squirm. Crowding them onto the ragged edge and keeping them there. But now I could see it wasn't going to work. They might crack up and be unable to do what they had to. They might feel I was just waiting for a chance to pay them off, that they had to get me before I got them.

I'd had to shake hands with Uncle Bud. I'd had to pull him off the spot I'd put him on, make him think that things were at least reasonably okay. And Fay, I'd have to do the same thing with her—if I could. Because the other wouldn't work. The other took more out of me than I had.

I couldn't beat them over the head without beating myself.

It was night, dark, when I finally thought things out. As good, I mean, as I could think them out. I got up and went downstairs, and I stood there in the yard a while, looking in through the back door of the house.

Fay and the boy were at the kitchen table. She was holding him on her lap, not eating anything herself. But it looked like he was eating quite a bit.

He finished after a few minutes. They left the kitchen, the boy holding on to her hand, and watching through the windows I saw her take him into the bedroom.

I went on inside. There was a lot of stuff left on the table—canned beans and boiled ham and half of a pie. So I warmed up the coffee, and started eating.

Fay came in, pulling the door shut behind her. I looked up and nodded.

"How's the boy doing? Did he eat his dinner all right?"

"Did he?" She shrugged. "Don't tell me you don't know."

I supposed she must have noticed me out in the yard. I said I'd just waited out there until the boy was through because I was afraid I might upset him.

"Uh-huh. Well, if that's all you were just doing, I'll just tell you that young Charles, heir apparent to the Vandeventer fortune, had a light repast consisting of one-half of a pie and approximately one pound of beans. Not to mention ham, bread, and perhaps another pound of beans by way of dessert."

"I see. I guess he must have been pretty hungry."

"Now, I'll just bet he was! It hadn't occurred to me, but I can see now that he must have been."

She'd brought a bottle in from the living room. A full one, so I guessed she must have finished the other one. Fay poured herself a drink, that mean little smile playing around her lips when she saw me frown.

"Yes, he must have been hungry," she continued. "And I must be thirsty. You have parted the clouds, Collie, and at last everything is clear to me."

"I want to say something. I've been thinking things over, and I think maybe I was wrong about today."

"Yes? You think so—*maybe?*"

"About you, not Uncle Bud. I know what he was planning to do, but you didn't have to be in on it. You'd've had to ride along with him after he'd done it, but you might not have known about it beforehand."

"Go on. I maybe didn't. I might not have." She nodded over her glass. "It's algebra isn't it? You multiply the two minuses, and it gives you a plus."

"Look, I— Did you or didn't you? Just tell me."

"Tell you? Oh, that's against the rules, Collie. When you have to ask another person for the answer, it doesn't count."

"Well . . . well, at least tell me this. About yesterday and you finding out about me. Could you—would it have been all right? I know how people feel about those things, but I was through the worst of it and if I could have just gone on . . ."

"Yes. So would I have cared to accompany you for the rest of the journey? Well—" Her eyes glinted. "Would I or wouldn't I? As I said before, my answer doesn't count."

I shoved my plate back. I poured coffee into my cup, slopping it over into the saucer.

Fay poured another drink of the whiskey.

"Aside from the rules, Collie, I can't answer you. The question is posed on circumstances that no longer exist. Before three this afternoon I could have answered it, and you would have believed me. You'd have had no reason not to. But after that, after your little set-to with Uncle Bud, and your flat accusation that I was—"

"All right!" I interrupted her. "Why do you have to keep harping on it? What would you have thought if you'd been in my place?"

"Exactly what you did, my friend. I implied as much at the time."

I got up suddenly and went to the door. I stood there, wanting to leave, feeling like I had to get away from her. And feeling and wanting just the opposite. Wanting, feeling—I didn't know just what. I didn't want her to think I was suspicious of her, but I didn't want her to think she could get away with a double-cross either. I didn't want to be afraid of her, or to have her afraid of me. I wanted . . .

I looked out into the yard, out at the raked-up piles of grass, withered heaps in the moonlight. And I knew that what I wanted, I wasn't going to get. It was gone. It couldn't be brought back to life any more than that mowed-down grass could.

"That door," Fay said. "If you go through it you'll find a walk and at the end of the walk there's a lane, and at the end of the lane there's a highway . . ."

"Yeah? That door is wide enough for two people."

"These two?"

"Look," I said. "I'm not sure I know what you want. You mean, just walk off and forget about the money? You're willing to forget the whole thing, if I am?"

"The money has nothing to do with the matter, Collie. After all, it was supposed to be purely a means to an end, wasn't it? Whether it would achieve that end—a happy partnership, we'll call it—depends largely on us."

"Well, sure, but—"

"So there's our door to life. Let's see if it's wide enough for both of us."

She got up and went into her bedroom. I listened to her moving around, wondering uneasily what she was up to. Because it should have been clear enough to me, but it wasn't.

It was almost twenty minutes before Fay came back, her face made up and her coat and hat on. She nodded to me, and started for the door. I was too startled to move for a second. Then, I jumped up and got in front of her.

"Wait a minute! Where are you going?"

"Going?" She smiled up at me. "Why, I'm going out."

"I said *where*? You've got nothing to see Uncle Bud about. You've got no business at Bert's place. So where else could you be going?"

Her smile drew in at the corners. She stepped back from me, just a step but it seemed to take her awfully far away, and held out her hand.

"I almost forgot. The car keys, Collie."

"But where—" I broke off. "Oh," I said. "You're . . . you're just going for a little ride? You want to get a breath of air?"

"The car keys, Collie."

I gave her the keys, sort of laying them in her hand without quite letting go. "What does this prove, Fay? You just get up without any warning and start to leave. I suppose it wouldn't have bothered you, if I'd done that?"

"Do you? Do you so suppose? Well, treasure the thought, my friend. Some wastrel who doesn't care about inflation may give you a penny for it."

She jerked the keys out of my hand, and left. Just before she started the car, I heard her laugh—angry and teasing. Or maybe disgusted and disappointed. I took a fast step toward the door, then I snatched up the whiskey bottle and went into the living room.

I sat down with my back to the windows. I made myself sit there, not moving or looking around until she'd driven away. But why I did it, I don't know. It didn't mean anything. Feeling like I did—wanting to stop her, worried about where she was going and what she might be doing—it meant just the opposite of what it should have meant.

We couldn't go through the door together. We couldn't walk together very far on the other side of the door. So she'd proved her point. . . . if that's what she'd meant to do. And how did I know that Fay had?

Maybe it had all been a build-up, a way of pointing me in one direction so she could move in another. Why not? Fay couldn't get me to clear out, and leave her and Uncle Bud or someone else with my share of the loot. So she'd picked up with another plan, another way of cutting me out of the deal. She'd know just how to go about it. Right from the beginning, she'd been able to get me so rattled and mixed up I didn't know what I was doing.

Sure, she'd sent me away that first time. But Fay must have known I'd come back. I didn't have any place else to go, and—

"Mister . . ." It was the boy, standing in the bedroom door. "Mister, I'm sick. I got to—to—"

His tiny body swayed, doubled at the waist. He put his hands over his mouth, and there was a gurgling sound. Then I swept him up in my arms and ran with him to the bathroom.

I wasn't quite fast enough. He was vomiting before I could get him over the toilet stool. The stuff gushed out of his mouth, splashing over the bathroom floor. Just when I thought there couldn't be anything left in him, it started coming out the other way.

"Sorry." Gasping for breath, he tried to apologize. "I'll—I'll clean it up, mister."

"No, you won't," I said. "Never mind, sonny. You just cut loose as much as you want to."

I had him sitting on the stool at the time. I was down in front of him, mopping and wiping with a towel. And there was something in his expression that stabbed through me like a knife.

"Y-You're not—m-mad at me?" he said.

"Mad?" I chucked him under the chin. "Hell, no, sonny! Why should I be mad at a little boy for being sick?"

He looked at me doubtfully. Apparently, he'd been expecting a spanking, and he still couldn't believe that he wasn't going to get one.

"Honest?" he said skeptically. "You're really not mad?"

"Honest. I'm not mad, and no one else is going to get mad. Because if they do—if anyone even looks like they're going to say a cross word to you—I'll, well they'd better not, that's all!"

He was sick; terribly sick. But a smile slowly spread over his face, and I think it was the most beautiful smile I have ever seen.

Then his arms went around my neck, and he pressed his face against mine. And the words he whispered to me . . . I guess they were the nicest I have ever heard.

"I like you, mister. I like you very much."

. . . It was around eleven o'clock when Fay got home. I'd dozed off in my chair, and I waked up when I heard the back door slam. There was another bang as she dropped a bag of groceries on the kitchen table. She came into the living room, threw her hat and coat into a chair, and sat down in another one.

She didn't look drunk; I mean, she didn't wobble or stagger. But you could see the booze in her eyes, see it in her tight twisted little smile.

"The rats are still in the harness," she said. "I'm saving the pumpkin to make a pie."

I didn't say anything. Right just then, I didn't trust myself to.

"That's pie without an *e*, Collie. You multiply it by the frammis, and it gives you Cinderella. Coach on, or would you like to try for the jackpot? If you win, you get a window to throw it out of."

"The boy's been sick, Fay. I've taken him to the bathroom a half a dozen times."

"My, my! Well, you just tell him he has to take you the next half dozen."

"Damn it, it's not funny! What the hell's the matter with you, anyway? I told you he's sick."

"And I heard you!" Her voice sharpened. "What do you want me to do about it, ring for Doctor Kildare?"

I told her she'd done too damned much already, stuffing a kid full of junk when he was already upset. "You must have known it would make him sick. You load him up on the worst stuff you could think of, beans and pie and—"

"Sure, I did!" she yelled. "I force-fed him, didn't I? I ran a hose down his throat and pumped it into him! I tried to kill him! Why the hell don't you say so?"

"Now, wait a minute. I didn't say—"

"Aah, shut up! Go file the point on your head. But just don't try to kid me. Don't tell me you hadn't thought of it."

I blinked. I didn't know what she was talking about. I'd been pretty mad when she first came in, pretty sore and worried, so I guess I'd talked kind of rough.

"You're not that stupid," said Fay. "Sure, you've thought of it. We've got him, haven't we? We collect just as much if he's dead, and we save ourselves a lot of trouble."

I shook my head. I just sat there shaking my head.

Fay grinned at me, her eyes narrowed. "Can't take it, huh? Well, in a case like that there'd seem to be only one logical alternative."

"You're drunk. You don't know what you're saying."

"Want to bet? Let's bet pumpkins. Yours looks pretty green from here, but I'm a sport."

She reached for the bottle on the table, and took a swig from it. She hefted it, studying me, two trickles of booze running down the corners of her mouth. Then, she shrugged and slammed it back on the table.

"To hell with it," she said. "To hell with you. I'm going to bed."

Fay pushed herself up from the chair, picked up her coat and hat. Wobbling a little now. That last jolt of whiskey had hit her hard.

"Midnight," she mumbled. "So it's the end of the ball. Li'l Cinderella's gotta crawl back under her cork. Well, what's layin' on your larynx, stupid?"

"Nothing had better happen to that boy," I said. "There'd sure better not anything happen to him."

"Yeah? Well, right back at you, brother rat. Paste it into your hat. Line that pumpkin with it."

"You heard me! You may be drunk, but you know what you're doing."

Her eyes flickered. Her face twisted suddenly, like maybe she was going to vomit. Then, she turned and staggered toward her bedroom door.

"Stupid," she mumbled. "S-s-stupid an' can't help it. H-he can't, but . . ."

Fay went through the door, kicking it shut with her foot.

I stayed where I was for a while afterwards. Thinking that the boy might need me to help him again, and just thinking in general. About myself, about Uncle Bud, about her. Thinking in circles, and not getting anywhere. That stuff she'd said about the boy, about it being better for us if he was dead. Maybe she was trying to chase me off with that talk, to scare me into leaving for my own good. Or maybe she was doing it for her—their—own good. Or maybe she really meant it. Or maybe she was just testing me out to see how I'd take it. And if they really planned on having him dead, and if I wouldn't go along with the plan . . .

Maybe. If. If and maybe.

How the hell was I going to know? How could you know

what people would do if they'd go in on a deal like this one?

I made myself stop thinking about it. My head just wouldn't take it any more, all that chasing around and around. So I started thinking about the little boy. Not the one we had, Charles Vanderventer III, but the first one. That little kid who was heading for Paris tonight.

I wondered if he'd meant what he kind of seemed to mean. Whether, you know, he'd been wise to what I was doing and had deliberately let me get away with it.

I guessed he hadn't. It was hard to be sure—he was such a sharp, fast-talking youngster—but I guessed he hadn't. I mean, he just couldn't have! No kid would have felt like that, felt that another kid would be better off kidnaped.

I turned the radio on low. The newscaster was just winding up his last broadcast for the night:

". . . No further developments in the Vanderventer case at this time. And now a few words about that plane disaster I mentioned a moment ago. The deluxe trans-Atlantic airliner crashed at La Guardia Airport, shortly after eleven tonight, when two of its motors failed simultaneously during the takeoff. All of the crew and all but three of the passengers were killed. Among the fatalities was ten-year-old Jacques Flannagan, son of motion-picture actor, Howard Flannagan of Hollywood, and Margot Flannagan Wentworth D'Arcy Holmes of Paris and London. In accordance with their divorce agreement, the boy spent six months a year with each parent. He had left this city earlier tonight, following a brief visit with his grandmother . . ."

13

That next day.
Just about everything happened that day. Just about everything seemed to go wrong.

It was the day the boy almost died. It was the day Bert tried to kill Uncle Bud. It was the day I robbed Doc Goldman's office. It was the day Fay tried to—to what?

Everything happened. Everything went wrong.

Everything got worse than it had been.

So maybe I'd better take it from the beginning. I'd better start with Fay shaking me awake. Yelling at me to get up, and me darting my hand under the pillow, and coming out with the automatic I'd taken off of Uncle Bud. I didn't mean to kill her, naturally—I hadn't got to that point then. It was just that I'd gone to bed late and gone to sleep a hell of a lot later, and when she— But let's go back to the beginning.

"Collie! Collie, *stop!*"

I heard her screaming from a long way off. Screaming my name, yelling for some guy named Collie to stop. And for a moment it meant nothing at all to me. It was just a voice, just a name; it was coming from just one more of the twisted, white faces that had swarmed around me all night long.

They meant nothing. The only thing that mattered was this thing that someone had put in my hand. Something hard and cold and heavy. I looked down at it while the screaming went on, not really looking because my eyes were open, but I couldn't see with them. I just knew I had it and that I must have it for a reason, and the only reason I could think of was—

"*Collie—don't!* D-DONT!"

"Huh? What?"

"The boy, Collie! H-he's—*put it down!*"

I saw that the face had a body. The two merged, then slid down the wall and into a chair. And my mind began to wake up. It moved up from the darkness slowly, patching up the past, trying to make the day something I would wake up to.

"Going to put the grass back," I mumbled. "Put everything back like it was. Wasn't very pretty, but . . . but . . ."

"Aaah, hell," she sobbed. "Aaah, damn it to hell."

My fingers loosened, and the gun dropped to the bed. I sat up, feeling the old sickness clutch at my stomach. I stared at her, rubbing the sleep out of my eyes. Hating her and myself and this whole world I'd had to come back to.

"What's the matter?" I said. "What's wrong with the boy? What did you do to him?"

"Do to him!" Fay's head jerked up. "Why, damn you, I—

Aaah, what's the use? He's sick, that's what's the matter. He looks like he's dying. I just woke up a few minutes ago, and I went right in to see how he was and he—h-he— He can't seem to get awake, Collie!"

"All right. Get back over there with him. Just stay there until I get over. Don't bother him or try to feed him."

"Feed him! How the hell could I?"

"Go on. Get out!"

Fay got out. I threw on my clothes, shoved the gun into my hip pocket, and ran down the stairs. It was noon. The hot sunlight hit me like a club, stirring up my stomach all over again. I stopped and was sick. I ran on a few steps and then I vomited again. I stood panting, bent over, waiting a few moments. But that seemed to do it for the time being. The sickness was gone as much as it was going to go. I ran on into the house and into the boy's bedroom.

Fay was in there with him. I brushed her out of the way, and bent down by his bedside. I studied him, listened to his breathing. I turned on the light and went down on my knees, bringing myself closer to him while I looked and listened.

His skin was flushed, hot, but damp looking. His eyes were partly open—sort of slitted. They were glazed, but he blinked a little when I passed my hand in front of them. He hardly seemed to breathe at all. His breath had a faint sweetish smell, and there was the same smell to his body. His pulse was pretty slow, but the beat wasn't bad. I mean it seemed fairly steady.

"Well?" Fay frowned at me. "Damn it, say something! Do something!"

"Turn the radio on. Get the newscast."

"Turn the radio on!"

"There ought to be something about this," I said. "About the boy. I think I know what's the matter, but I want to make sure."

She turned it on. A minute or two later Uncle Bud arrived from town with an armload of newspapers, so we got the word both ways at once. And it was just what I'd thought. I was right about the boy, and I wished to God that I wasn't.

I covered him up good. Then, I got a spoon and a cup, and fed him a few sips of lukewarm water. That didn't seem to help much, but it was about all I could do. I turned the light off and went into the living room.

Fay was working on a water glass full of whiskey. Uncle Bud, who also had a drink, was settled back in a chair taking things easy. He'd been all pepped up when he arrived. The family had got the ransom note, and they'd asked the police to stay out of the deal—to "cooperate," as the newspapers put it. Just to keep hands off, and let them pay the ransom and get the boy back. And it looked like the police were going to let them have their way.

I sat down, looking from Fay to Uncle Bud. He wiped the pleased grin off his face, turned on a sympathetic frown.

"Diabetes," he said. "Now, that's bad, that is. Who'd've ever thought he'd have a thing like that?"

I could think of a couple of people who might have thought it. Who damned well ought to have known about it. Because, hell, Uncle Bud knew everything else about the kid, didn't he? He and Fay had been kicking the kidnaping around for months, and he'd been digging into the boy's and the family's background even before that. So why wouldn't he have found out about this?

But—well, maybe he hadn't. If the kid was taken care of properly, if he was kept on a strict diet and got the right amount of rest and exercise and so on, the disease wouldn't bother him much. He wouldn't need too much in the way of actual medical treatment. Then, maybe his family was touchy on the subject—like some people are touchy about anything in the way of sickness or weakness—and they'd tried to keep the trouble hushed up.

It could have been that way; the family keeping quiet, the boy not too bad off. Anyway, regardless of whether Fay and Uncle Bud had known or not, it didn't change anything. And there was no point in trying to pin them down.

"Yes, sir," said Uncle Bud. "Yes, sir, it's sure a shame, a nice little boy like that. I guess you know quite a bit about the stuff, huh, Kid?"

I nodded. "People in mental institutions have it the same as anyone else. They don't always get treated for it, but they have it."

"Yeah? Now, that's sure a shame. I don't suppose you—uh—you wouldn't have any ideas about what we ought to do?"

Fay laughed and choked on her drink. I said I had a pretty good idea of what we ought to do, but I didn't have the stuff to do it with.

"I've worked as an orderly in several places. They never have enough help, so when they find a patient that's intelligent, they—"

Fay let out another whoop. I looked at her, not saying anything. Just sitting and staring until she was all through laughing. She cut it off pretty fast. She raised her drink, holding it up in front of her face, and I went on staring a moment longer.

"The boy's in a diabetic coma," I explained. "It isn't a bad one, and I think he'll pull through it. I think he can be pulled through it. But if he is, if we get him through this, he's practically a cinch to slide into another one. And as weak and run down as he is . . ."

"Yeah," Uncle Bud frowned. "I guess all that starch and sugar was pretty bad for him, huh?"

"It's a wonder it didn't kill him."

"Well, maybe it will yet!" Fay snatched up the bottle, re-filled the water glass. "Maybe I'll get him next time! Why, the h-hell don't you say what you mean?"

"Now, now." Uncle Bud shook his head. "So what do you drink, Kid?"

"He needs insulin. He'll die if he doesn't get it."

"Yeah? Well, let's see. I know a few places, drug stores where they ain't too particular if they know a guy. But to do it now, when it's in all the papers and the heat's on . . . It'd be asking for trouble, really begging for it. I'm out in front on this deal, and if the word leaked out . . ."

He was right. Even someone with a prescription would probably be checked on now.

"I just don't see what we can do, Kid. I don't hardly know what we could do if we had the stuff. I mean, you've been around people with the disease—worked with the doctors—but the papers and radio don't say how much of the insulin the boy's been getting."

"They couldn't. The dosage would vary according to his condition. I'd have to kind of feel around for what he needed, start off with the minimum dose and work up."

"Uh-huh. I see . . ."

He went on asking questions, sort of aimlessly it seemed to me. Not paying too much attention to the answers . . . He was all for helping the boy, y'know. He loved children, Uncle Bud did. But it looked to him like there was every chance of harming him rather than helping him. After all, I wasn't a doctor. I just naturally couldn't be sure of whether I was doing the right thing or not. And with the boy as bad off as he was, just one little wrong move would probably push him over the line.

"You see my point, Kid. And it ain't that I don't think you mean well."

"I see your point," I said. "I see yours, all right. But maybe you don't see mine. If there's no trouble, like we're all hoping, we don't need the boy alive. In fact, it's a lot less risky for us if he isn't alive. They have to take our word for it that we're going to return him. We get the money either way; and without him around as evidence—someone we might get caught with, and who'll be telling all he knows afterwards—we'd be a lot safer. But . . ."

I broke off for a moment. Because it was hard to talk this way, so cold-blooded and everything. But I figured it was the best way to talk. I didn't know what was in their minds, whether they were just putting on an act or whether they really didn't want the boy to die. But I knew that if they did want him dead, they'd see that he was. They'd arrange it somehow sometime. And the only way I could stop them was to prove that it just wouldn't be smart.

"Go on, Kid," Uncle Bud nodded. "Of course, I wouldn't want a nice little boy like that to die. But if we just can't help it, well, it's like you say. It would work out pretty nice for us."

"I didn't say that. I mean, I said it but I was just pointing out how you might look on it. Me, I don't look on it that way. That family has half of the money in the state. If they don't get the boy back, they'll probably spend every nickel of it running us down. But then—well, suppose things don't come off as smooth as we hope they will and we got caught. It would sure be a lot better for us if the boy was alive. Even if he wasn't, if we could just show that we'd done everything we could do for him, it would, be a lot better."

Uncle Bud frowned, chewing his lip. He hesitated, nodded slowly. "Yeah." He sighed. "I guess you're right, Kid. We sure got to do what we can, even if it don't work out right. But how can we get that insulin?"

"Doc Goldman," I said impatiently. "He comes back to his office at two, and he's there until five. He doesn't take any office patients after that time. If someone could call him just before five, get him out on a fake call, I could have a good look around."

"I get it, I get you, Kid. There wouldn't be anyone there? You could get in and out all right?"

"Easy. He never locks the place up. I know right where he keeps everything. The chances are he'd never know that anyone had been there."

"Swell. Well, that settles that then." He got up and put his glass on the table. "Now, I'm going to be tied up right until about five. I got to keep right on top of this deal, you know, keep in touch with everything that's happening. So I'll just run along now, and you can come in later."

"Come in?" said Fay. "How's he going to get there? You think I'm going to be stuck out here without a car?"

"Why not?" I said. "What do you want with a car?"

"What do you think, stupid? I want to take the tires off and make myself a girdle!"

"But why—"

"She's right, Kid," Uncle Bud broke in hastily. "Everything's going to be jake, but still the little lady'll feel a lot easier with a car. I know I would. So you come in with me."

I guessed I probably would, too. Anyway, with Fay dead set on keeping the car, there was no use in arguing about it.

I ran over to the garage and got my coat and tie. He was waiting in his car for me when I came down, and we started for the city.

He'd dumped the station wagon with a salvage dealer pal of his, he said. A guy that bought hot cars and wrecked them for their parts. Of course, he went on casually, he hadn't been able to get any money for it—only a few bucks, that is. The guy was just trying to be friendly, y'know, just being a pal. So it wouldn't have been right to take money from him.

I grinned to myself. Kind of embarrassed for him, for

Uncle Bud, I mean. Kind of ashamed for him. Here he was, about to pull down a hundred thousand dollars, his share of the ransom, and he couldn't pass up the smallest chance to chisel someone. It was the way he was made. He'd rather chisel a dollar than earn a hundred.

"That's the way I am, Kid," he continued. "I play straight with my pals, and I like to have them play straight with me. Like take us for example. Now, we've had our little spats and misunderstandings maybe, but they don't amount to nothing. We all like and trust each other, we're pals, y'know. Everything's on the up and up with us, with no one holding out anything on another one."

He paused, studying me slyly out of the corner of his eyes. I didn't say anything, and he went on.

"Now, take that little yarn you told me, Kid. I was kind of hurt at the time, but I know you were just joking. Why, hell you wouldn't have passed that card I gave you to someone else! You'd be afraid the party might ask you some questions, try to cut himself in maybe. That's right, ain't it?" He laughed and nudged me with his elbow. "You were just having a little joke with your old Uncle Bud?"

I shrugged. I still didn't say anything.

"Well?" he said, his laugh trailing off. "What about it Kid?"

"What about it?" I said.

"Well, uh, what I was saying, dammit. I said you wouldn't have done it, because you'd be afraid that— that—" He broke off abruptly, his face falling. "Oh," he said. "The guy ain't in a position to ask questions, huh? Or maybe you promised him a nice piece of change?"

I shrugged again. He was doing a lot better with the answers than I could.

"But that's not giving me a fair shake, Kid! Suppose something happens that's not my fault? I play it straight with you, but someone else pulls something and this guy cracks down on me!"

I still didn't say anything. He looked at me uncertainly.

"You wouldn't put me on a spot like that, Kid. You're a guy that likes to play fair, and you'd have seen it wasn't fair. You didn't do it . . . did you?"

I smiled at him. He waited a moment, and then he

grumbled something under his breath. And for the rest of the ride he didn't have much to say either.

It was two-thirty when he pulled up at a bar on the edge of the business district. He said he'd pick me up there in a couple hours, and I got out and went in.

It was a dingy, dimly lit place with a bar and lunch counter up front and a few pool tables in the back. There were only a couple of customers, and they drifted out while I was having a sandwich and some beer. I bought another beer, picked up an afternoon newspaper from the counter and went over to a booth.

There was a big picture of the boy on the front page. There were pictures of his parents and the playground matron and the chauffeur; practically everyone that could be tied into the case in any way. And just about the whole paper was filled with news of the kidnaping. Or, I should say, stories about it Because they hadn't been able to dig up much of anything new.

A ransom note had been received. The kidnapers had demanded a quarter of a million dollars for the boy's return. How, where—and *when*—the money was to be paid, "had not been revealed." The details were a secret between the police and the family.

And, of course, Uncle Bud.

I went through the stories carefully, making sure that I didn't miss anything. I took them apart word by word, and they still added up to nothing. But for me it was a kind of uncomfortable nothing . . . The cops wouldn't reveal the details about the ransom payment, but there could be more than one reason for that. It could be that they just didn't know any to reveal. Uncle Bud said that they did. He'd said that the family had shown them the ransom note to make sure that they wouldn't accidently mix up in the case. Get in the way of the pay-off, you know, and endanger the boy's life.

That sounded reasonable enough, because the boy wasn't to be released until twenty-four hours after the money had been paid. The cops might grab the guy at the pay-off, but it was likely to get the boy killed if they did. So—so, it sounded reasonable. It was the way Uncle Bud had planned things, the way he'd explained them to Fay and me, and everything seemed to be going according to plan. So perhaps everything was okay. But I was beginning to have some doubts.

It was Uncle Bud's job to pick up the money. It was his job to keep track of what the police knew. And if they didn't know how or where or when the ransom was to be paid—if they were "cooperating" because they had to, it made a nice setup for him. Or even if the cops did know, it was still just about as nice. If they weren't ready to cooperate yet, he'd just wait until they were.

And only he knew exactly when that would be. Only he knew how much time the Vanderventers had been given to come across. He'd told Fay and me it was seventy-two hours, but it could be less. He could collect the dough one night—tomorrow night, say—and be out of the country the next morning.

I got another beer, and brought it over to the booth. I wondered how, if he was planning a fast one, I could head him off . . . Demand to pick up the money myself? Uh-uh, I guessed not. He could send me into a police trap. Then, while I was getting bumped off, he could grab the money and skip. He wouldn't need to worry about that "friend" of mine then. That "friend" couldn't make him any more trouble than I could.

Fay? Should I wise her up, see if we could work out something together? Uh-uh, again. She might be in on Uncle Bud's scheme. She might have plans of her own. Anyway, and regardless of whether she was on the level with me or not, it wasn't safe to tell her anything. Not after she'd turned on me like she had. Not with her boozing like she was. She might do something crazy and dangerous, just for the hell of it.

I didn't know what I should do. Hell, I didn't even know whether I should even be thinking about doing anything. Everything was working out like we'd planned, wasn't it? The only thing that had really changed was me—my mind. I was getting so confused and mixed-up that nothing looked straight to me, and any little thing made me suspicious. Anything or nothing. If things went one way I didn't like them, and if they went another way I didn't like them. And—and it had to stop! If it didn't, if people didn't stop worrying me, coming at me from every direction, pushing and crowding and . . .

A band seemed to tighten around my head. I closed my eyes, and for a moment I just wasn't there. There was nothing but blackness with me floating away on it.

After a while the band got looser, and the blackness faded away. I gulped down the rest of the beer fast. And in a minute or two I was all right again. Or as right as I was going to be.

I lighted a cigarette. I heard the screen door slam, and I started to peer out of the booth. Then, I jerked my head back, and raised the newspaper up in front of my face. Because it was Uncle Bud, all right; he'd come right on the dot of four-thirty. But he had someone with him—Bert.

 .

Uncle Bud was in front. Bert was walking right on his heels, kind of moving him along with his body. The bartender glanced at them casually and went back to polishing glasses. Uncle Bud was looking straight ahead, his face a white blur in the dimness; and Bert was looking straight at the back of Uncle Bud's neck.

They passed down the length of the bar. They went down the long lane at the side of the pool tables. They reached the rear of the place, and Uncle Bud stopped in front of the rest room door. Bert nudged him. He said something to him, gave him another nudge.

Uncle Bud opened the door. Bert shoved him through it and went in after him.

I was on my feet the moment the door closed. I carried my beer bottle over to the bar, took a step or two toward the front door, then turned around and headed back toward the rear.

Just short of the rest room, I turned and glanced behind me. The bartender was still at his glass-polishing. No one else had come in. I hurried on, walking on the balls of my feet and paused outside the rest room door.

Keeping an eye on the bartender. Listening.

"Cheatin' bastard!" Bert was saying. "Thought I'd never catch up with you, huh? Well, I'm the last guy you'll ever chisel! I'm gonna—"

"Naw, naw, B-Bert!" Uncle Bud gave a kind of stuttering gasp. "You got to listen to me! You got to give me a little time! J-just give me—*No!*"

There was a *click*—a knife coming open. And a slow scuffing of feet as, I imagined, Bert moved toward him and Uncle Bud backed away.

"Naw, naw!" He gasped again. "A little time B-Bert, j-just give me a little time an' you'll get every penny! I swear it, B-B—"

I eased the door open a crack, saw that Bert's back was toward me. I pulled it open a little further, watching him, watching that long sharp knife in his hand.

"I'll give you somethin'!" The blade trembled and he grunted for emphasis. "I'll give you all the time in the world and the next one, too, you rotten, chiseling, no-account son-of-a-bitch!"

He brought the knife up suddenly. Uncle Bud sort of moaned and sobbed. Then I threw the door back and went in.

Bert didn't have time to turn around. I had one all set for him, a hard right hook, and he got it in the back of the neck.

The knife flew out of his hand. He pitched forward, striking his head on the stained iron urinal, then fell sprawling face-down to the floor.

Uncle Bud sagged against the wall, pawing the sweat from his white face. He looked down at Bert, straightened up suddenly and kicked him as hard as he could in the head.

"Going to give it to me, were you?" he spat. "Well, damn you, I'll—!" He aimed another kick. I shoved him back against the wall, then grabbed him by the arm and hustled him toward the door.

"Come on! Come on, dammit! We've got to get out of here!"

"B-but—" He tried to hang back. "He was going to kill me! You saw him, Kid. H-he was goin' to—" He took a deep shuddering breath, and the glaze went out of his eyes. "Yeah," he said. "Yeah, sure, Kid."

We got out of there. A few blocks away, we stopped at another bar and he put down a couple of fast drinks. He needed them. He had the shakes so bad that you could almost hear him rattle.

"Hell, Kid," he said, as we drove away from the place, "I never got such a scare in my life! I didn't dare turn my head to see if you were there. I was afraid maybe you'd stepped out for a few minutes."

"Yeah. Where'd he pick you up, anyway?"

"That's what I don't know! That's what gave me such a jolt! I'd parked my car and was just starting through the door of the joint, and there the murdering son-of-a-bitch was! Right behind me with that knife in my back. Hell, he seemed to come from nowhere! It was like he'd dropped down out of the sky!"

"Then he could have been tagging you around for quite a while."

"He could have been, but it doesn't seem likely. It looks like I'd have spotted him if he had. No, I figure he must have just been there in the neighborhood and he picked me up when I got out of the car." He shook his head, stared frowning through the windshield. "I hope it was that way, anyhow. I mean, that he just happened to bump into me accidentally. I'd sure hate to think that . . ."

I nodded. I'd have hated to think it, too. I didn't care about Uncle Bud particularly, because a guy like he was—a guy that had taken everyone he could, that had caused all the misery he must have caused—was long overdue for the cemetery. But this would be a bad time for him to go there; and he'd be going there pretty fast if things were like they might be.

"I wonder," he said, worriedly. "I know a hell of a lot of people, and it could be that he's buddies with some of the same ones. He might have someone keeping an eye on me—several people, maybe—tipping him off every time they run into me anywhere. Why, hell, it could be and I wouldn't know it! All the people I've met, had dealings with, y'know, I don't always remember 'em myself!"

He was getting the shakes all over again. I told him there was probably nothing to worry about. After all, Bert had been gunning for him for quite a while, but he hadn't caught up with him until today.

"It was just an accident," I said. "He just happened to be in that neighborhood at the same time you were. If he had any help, he'd've tagged you before this."

"Well . . ." He hesitated. "Well, maybe. It kind of looks that way, don't it? Of course, he may be just now deciding to crack down. It's been quite a while since I skinned him—since we had this little misunderstanding, I mean."

"What about that bar?" I said. "Are you in there every day?"

"Kind of on schedule, you mean? Uh-uh, not me, Kid. Not your old Uncle Bud." He winked at me, grinning. "I don't do things that way. I move around. Even with living quarters, I don't keep any of 'em more than a few weeks."

"No one knew you were going to be there at the bar today? You didn't mention it to anyone?"

"Uh-uh. Not a soul. Well, I may have mentioned it to Fay, but no one else. Yeah, Kid," he pushed his hat back, began to relax, "I guess it's like you say. It was just one of them things, just an accident."

I had a hunch that it wasn't—that someone had tipped Bert off, and that someone would tip him off again. That they'd keep doing it until Bert managed to nail him. But it was only a hunch; Uncle Bud was jumpy enough already, and we still had things to do.

It was almost five o'clock when we stopped at a drug store a few blocks from Doc Goldman's house. I sat down at the counter and bought a coke, while he put in the phony call from a booth phone.

He came out of the booth, paused at my side a moment. "Okay, Kid. He fell for it. I'll be back for you as soon as he leaves."

He drove off. About ten minutes later, when I was finishing my second coke, he pulled up in front again.

He gave me a sharp-eyed look as I climbed into the car. "You look pretty peaked, Kid. How you holding up with all this, anyway?"

"All right. I'm all right."

"Well, uh, isn't all this nervous strain and excitement pretty hard on you? I know you're not really cra— I mean, you've just got a little nervous trouble. But—"

"Don't count on it." I turned around in the seat and stared at him. "Don't try to force me into it. Because if I do crack up, it won't be nice for anyone around me."

"Aah, now, Kid." He looked hurt. "Ain't we pals? Didn't you save my life today?"

"I'm all right. I'm going to go right on being all right, and no one had better try to trim me or double-cross me."

"Sure. Sure, Kid," he said hastily. "I was just concerned for you was all."

He let me out in front of Doc's place, and headed back to the drug store to wait for me. I took a quick glance around, and started up the walk.

The house was on the outskirts of the city—I guess I mentioned that before. There were two vacant lots between his house and the next one, and there were no houses at all on the other side of the street. I could be seen, of course. The people in that nearest place could see me if they happened to look that way. But if they did, I guessed they wouldn't think anything of it. They'd be used to seeing people come and go from Doc's house. I'd be just one more, another patient.

I went up the steps and across the porch. Then I opened the door and went in. That was the reception room there, the room the door opened into. The living quarters were on through to the rear, and his office and lab were on the right.

I looked around, and everything looked just as I remembered it. The chairs sitting around the walls. The little table stacked with magazines. The rug in the middle of the carpet to cover up a worn spot. The dime-store ash trays. The—

I couldn't go any further for a minute. I just had to stand there looking, feeling kind of good—safe and comforted—in one way, and pretty lousy in another. It was like coming home and pulling some dirty trick.

But I had to do it. I was doing it for the boy, not myself. So I crossed the reception room, and opened the office door.

And bumped smack into Doc Goldman.

He had his hat on. He'd been coming through the door from the other side, and he was just about as startled as I was. Which was plenty, believe me.

I tried to speak, to smile, but my mouth seemed to be in a knot. I didn't know what in the hell to do, and all I could think of was that he'd caught me red-handed, right in the act of breaking in on him.

I backed up a step. I mumbled something, God only knows what, and I was just about to turn and run.

But by then he was over his start.

"Collie! Collie, my friend!" He grabbed my hand and wrung it. "I'm sorry I didn't hear you come in. I got a flat on my car right around the corner, and I just ran back to call a cab."

"Oh." I began to breathe easier. For a moment I'd thought that Uncle Bud had tried to trick me. "Well, if you're going out—"

"No, no. It'll take a few minutes for the cab to get here. How have you been anyway? Come on in the lab and let me get a look at you."

He herded me into the laboratory, made me lie down on the examination table. He went on talking, asking questions, as he took my pulse and rested his hand on my forehead.

I said that I was still living at Mrs. Anderson's. She'd got over the shock of finding out about me, and now things were just like they had been.

"Well, that's fine, wonderful. I know how it must have seemed to you at the time, Collie. I can't tell you how blue I felt after you'd called me."

"I'm sorry about that. I didn't mean any of that stuff I said."

"Of course, you didn't. Not that there wasn't a certain amount of truth in it. But you understand, now, don't you, Collie? You see that she had to be told?"

"She had to all right. But it would have been a lot better if I'd told her right in the beginning."

"Yes? Well, anyway, we've got it all over with now, haven't

we? Now, if you'll just relax, just let yourself go limp . . ."

He dug his fingers into my biceps. He raised one of my arms and shook it, watching the movement of my hand. Then, he slid a light refractor onto his head and bent over me, pulling the lids back from my eyes.

"Uh-uh. Not that way, Collie. Look straight at me . . ."

He stared into first one eye, then the other. My eyes began to water and he let me rest them for a moment, and then he went on staring. At last, he straightened and took off the refractor. He stood frowning down at me, slapping the shiny metal disc against the palm of his hand.

"Not good, Collie. Not good at all. You're a lot more tense than you were the first night I met you."

"Yeah? I mean, I am? I feel fine."

"Like hell you do. What's bothering you? And don't tell me there isn't anything."

"Well, I—there isn't anything now, but there was. Mrs. Anderson took what you told her pretty hard. She's all right now, but I guess I'm still kind of upset."

"Kind of is hardly the phrase for it. And it doesn't quite add up for me, Collie. You were very far down in the dumps; the pendulum was right at its lowest point. Even without the situation ending reasonably happy—as you indicate it did—you should have been on the upswing by this time."

"Well, anyway it's like I told you. Everything is all right."

A horn honked in the street. His taxi. He hesitated, fidgeting.

"I guess I'll have to run, Collie, but— Can you wait here for me? I shouldn't be gone more than an hour."

"I don't know. I'd sure like to, but, well, Mrs. Anderson drove me into town tonight. There was some friends she had to see, and I guess I'll have to leave whenever she stops back by."

"You tell her to wait for you, Collie." He put his hat back on. "Tell her I'd like to see her, too. Will you do that?"

The horn honked again. I told him I didn't think she could wait; she'd probably be in a hurry.

"Well, wait by yourself then. I'll drive you home myself."

"I can't. I mean—well, I don't think I can. You see, I—I—"

"Yes?" he said. "Yes, Collie?" And then his expression

changed, became kind of a no-expression, and he turned and started for the door. "I'll have to run now. You stay if you can, Collie."

He hurried out. The front door slammed, and a moment later I heard the cab drive off.

I eased a hand under my right hip. I turned carefully, grabbing the gun just as it fell to the table. The damned thing had slipped when I'd laid down. If Doc had shifted me around any, he'd've seen it.

I shoved it back into my pocket. I boosted myself off the table and went to work on the medicine chest. It was a tall steel cabinet with six big drawers and about a dozen little drawers inside of each of the six. They were all unlocked. The only thing Doc locked up was his narcotics, and they were in the office safe.

I took a two-c.c. syringe and a couple of hypodermic needles—two in case one got broken. I went on looking, working fast, jerking the drawers in and out, until I found the insulin. It was the regular type, but there were only two vials of it, two of those glass, 400-unit, 10-c.c. tear-drop tubes. I hesitated, staring down at the little crystal-clear tubes. Then I laid them on the table with the hypodermic syringe and the needles and went back to the cabinet. The drawer labels might be haywire. Doc had a pretty big practice and no one to help him. And sometimes he mixed things up.

I started at the top of the cabinet again, and worked down. Taking it slower this time, looking carefully through each drawer. I worked from the top to the bottom, not missing a bet. And then, well, that was it. There was just the twenty c.c.'s. There wasn't any more, and this would have to do. It didn't look like it, but it could be more than enough to get the boy out of it and keep him going awhile. Actually, I really didn't know. I didn't know a lot of things.

I got a paper towel from the sink and wrapped the stuff up. I left the house, worried about getting what seemed so little and worried about taking that little. Doc was sure to miss it—his entire supply. All I could hope was that he wouldn't need it any time soon.

Uncle Bud was waiting in front of the drug store. We started for the house, and I told him my doubts. It didn't seem to exactly break his heart.

"Might not be enough, huh? Well, that's sure a shame. But you did your best, Kid. We all did our best."

I looked straight ahead, not saying anything. He took his hand off the wheel and gave me a little pat on the back.

"Now, don't you take it to heart, Kid. It's too bad, sure, but these things always work out for the best. It's like we were saying this morning, you know. We sure don't want that nice little boy to die, but it might not be too bad for us if he did."

"Yeah, that's right, isn't it? I guess that kind of slipped my mind."

"Why, sure. So cheer up, huh?" He gave me a nudge. "This may be a good break. Of course, we'll hope this'll be enough."

"Well, we can't be sure that it won't be," I said. "It might just do it. It might keep him alive for another couple of days, anyway, maybe a lot longer. I don't know."

"Yeah? But you said—"

"I said he'd probably need more. In his condition, I'm not sure this'll even halfway put him back on his feet. But it could keep him alive until after we get the money."

"Well . . ." He shrugged. "So we got nothing to worry about either way, have we?"

I nodded, shook my head. And it looked to me like he'd said a lot in that last sentence. Fay might want the boy dead, or she might want him to live. I didn't know which. But Uncle Bud—he'd given himself away. He wanted to keep Fay and me satisfied, to keep us from doing anything that would upset the apple cart. Aside from that, he didn't care what happened to the boy. And there was just one reason why he didn't.

He was going to skip with the money. When the storm broke, he'd be a long way off.

Or, anyway, he thought he would.

16

The boy was conscious, but he was awfully weak. His kidneys had been moving all day, trying to get rid of the sugar that his system couldn't burn. He was too weak to even whisper. I asked him how he felt, and his lips moved a little but no words came out.

Uncle Bud had left. He just couldn't be around anything like this, he said; anyone getting a needle stuck in them. It made him sick to his stomach, and anyway he had things to do in town.

Using a fork, I lifted a needle from the pan of water boiling on the stove. Then I fitted it to the hypodermic syringe and jabbed it into the rubber-capped tip of one of the 10-c.c. vials. I pulled back the plunger carefully. The syringe held two c.c.'s, and I wasn't sure of the minimum dosage for a seven-year-old child, a mighty sick one at that. But I figured he needed a good jolt.

Still, giving him too much at one time could be bad—even fatal. I remembered from the mental hospitals that one cubic centimeter was equal to 80 units. The label on the tubes said this was 400-unit, regular insulin; I knew this had to do with the concentration, but— Well, I had to admit it. I was scared and confused, but I had to go through with it and hope for the best.

I lifted the boy's limp arm and Fay, who had been watching from the doorway, frowned. "That's not right, is it? I've always gotten shots in the left arm."

I shook my head, not answering her; concentrating on the boy. He gave a little jump when the needle went in. Fay jumped, too, standing right behind me, and of course that gave me a start. I gave him the full two centimeters, more than I'd meant to, but then I'd been startled. I took out the needle and waited. I watched his face carefully for a reaction, but there was none. So I refilled the syringe with another two c.c.'s, inserted the needle into his arm, and gave him more.

He jumped and she jumped and I jumped. I put the needle down, looked at the boy, and now there was a definite reaction. He shuddered suddenly, took a long, shivering breath. His face turned red, and he burst out all over with sweat. He really felt that one.

I was elated that he'd come out of it, overcome with doubts that I'd given him an overdose, and then suddenly confident that I knew what I was doing. It was like it should have been, like it often was as I remembered, and I knew just what to do about it. But I didn't get the chance. I'd just snatched up the bowl of thick sugar-water and started to spoon it down the boy, when Fay yelled and knocked it out of my hand.

"You don't know what you're doing! You're crazy! You—you—!"

I jumped up, and grabbed her by the shoulders. "But I know what *you're* doing! And now you're through doing it!" I shoved her out of the room. I ran her backwards through the doorway, and slammed her down hard in a chair. "Now, stay there! If you foul me up again, I'll—I'll—"

I raced into the kitchen, threw together another bowl of sugar and water. I ran back into the bedroom with it, mixing it on the way, and began feeding it to the boy.

It was all he needed. Something to cushion the shock of the insulin. I held him up with one arm, shoving the sugar into him as fast as I could move the spoon. His breathing eased, there were no more of those shuddering gasps. It leveled off, became even and effortless. The sweating stopped, and the red went out of his face.

I lowered him to the pillow. He looked up at me wide-eyed—still scared, naturally; frightened at being here and lonesome for his own home—but feeling a lot better. Feeling so much better than he had that he couldn't help smiling feebly.

I smiled back at him. His eyes drifted shut, and he fell asleep. I stayed there with him a while, watching to see if there was a delayed reaction. There wasn't any, though, so I turned off the light and went into the living room.

Fay was right where I'had put her. I fixed myself a drink, and sat down. "He's all right. You can go in and look at him if you want to."

"I can, huh?" Fay looked grim.

"He's all right, and he's going to stay that way. I—it just makes good sense, Fay. You ought to see that. The better he is when he gets back to his folks, the better it'll be for us."

She grimaced. Her hand went out for the whiskey bottle and tilted it over her glass.

"When," she said dully. "You mean if, don't you?" Then, before I could answer her, "How long is that stuff you gave him going to last?"

"Long enough. I think it will, anyhow."

"Sure. You *think*. But you don't know, do you? All you know is that we've got him on our hands—a kid that's liable to go on us at any time. A kid that's got his picture in every paper in the country. We can't beat it with him, and we can't leave without him. We just have to sit here, hanging onto a keg of dynamite, and hope that lightning won't strike us."

"Have you got any better ideas?"

"Skip it. Forget it. I'll be screwy myself if I talk to you much longer."

I went out into the kitchen, and made a couple of sandwiches. I ate one of them and carried the other back into the living room.

She watched me as I began to eat, then laughed a kind of tired laugh. "Poor Collie. They may hang him, but he'll fill his stomach first."

"With food," I said pointedly.

"Mmm?" she frowned. Then, she laughed again. "Very good. Too damned good. It was things like that—that sort of thing that threw me off. You were so sharp sometimes that I didn't see how . . ."

"Yeah?"

"Never mind. That's the way it was. This is the way it is."

"I don't know what the doctor told you about me," I said. "Exactly what. But I'd like to know."

"Then I'll fill you in on the important points. He told me that with the right kind of environment and the right kind of associates you'd be all right. You were well on the road to recovery, and you'd soon be at the end of it. On the other hand—" She hesitated. "On the other hand . . ."

"Well?"

"Why bother with the rest of it? The unreasoning suspicion, the very-dangerous-if-aroused part. Let's just say that it's my fault, and I'm sorry. But that doesn't change anything. I can't let it change anything."

"Look, Fay. If I just knew what you wanted, if you'd just talk straight, maybe I could . . ."

"Ditto. Double ditto, you might say, since your background is considerably more ominous potentially than mine. No." She held up a hand. "Let's don't keep hashing it over. Because it gets a little messier each time, and I get a little sorrier for you. Just tell me one thing if you can. How long are you absolutely sure the boy will last without proper medical treatment?"

"I gave him proper treatment. Maybe you don't think so, but—"

"Now, don't go touchy on me, Collie! You know what I mean, so answer the question."

"Well, with the insulin I gave him and the way it took hold he's sure to be all right for another twenty-four hours."

"You sound so positive."

I had fooled her with my confident air so I ignored her remark. "He can eat something tomorrow and that'll help. A poached egg, maybe a little lean meat, and some milk."

She nodded, leaned back in her chair yawning. "Excuse me, it's not the whiskey, but the company. Why don't you take yourself off, doctor? I think they're calling for you in the annex."

I said I guessed I would turn in. I was pretty tired, and the boy should sleep soundly for the rest of the night. She looked at me absently, not saying anything, so I carried my plate out into the kitchen and left.

Quite a breeze had sprung up, and it was actually kind of cold. But I left the front window of the apartment open. It faced on the driveway, and if she started the car or if anyone came up the lane I'd be sure to hear it. I—well, I just didn't know, you see. I didn't know why anyone might be coming up there, or why she might try to drive off. I didn't know what might happen or why, so I just had to try to look out for everything.

I undressed. I started to slide the gun under my pillow, but then I thought that might be something else to look out for. She knew I kept it there, so maybe I'd better put it some place else.

I looked around. Finally, I pulled the reading stand a little closer to the bed, laid the gun on top of it, and covered it with an opened magazine. That looked natural enough, like I'd been reading the magazine and laid it down open to hold my place. I could reach the gun as fast as if it was under my pillow.

I turned off the light, and went to bed.

I fell alseep right away. Thirty minutes later I waked up, still dead tired, but too tense to relax. I got a drink of water and smoked a couple cigarettes. Afterwards I dozed a little, and then came awake again. Restless and uneasy. My nerves drawn into a knot. My mind going around and around.

Uncle Bud. I knew what he was going to pull, so what was I going to do about it? How was I going to stop him? I knew I had to—even if didn't know why I had to—but I had no idea how to go about it.

He was there in my mind; there was a big picture of him there. Hat pushed back on his smooth gray head, an easy smile on his face, his eyes warm and friendly. I could see him as plain as day, hear his soft, restful voice. I concentrated and I could hear him talking about—about—I listened carefully, clearing my mind of everything but him, and the words came through at last—about the ransom pay-off.

He told me about it all over again, patiently, beaming at me. And all the time laughing to himself:

"Yeah, I know, Kid. That's the way it's usually done, and that's the way so many guys get knocked off. They go way to hell out in the country somewhere—and they fix it up so the money will be thrown out of a car or some deal like that. They think they're safe because there's no one else around, but that's just why they ain't safe. How do they know what's off in the woods, or behind a hill? How do they know the whole damned area ain't been staked out? You see what I mean, Kid? They actually give the cops a setup. If there's no one around but one guy, that guy has to be it . . . So we won't do it that way. I won't. The way I'll work it—

The money would be left at the railroad station checkroom for a "Mr. Whitcomb." A messenger—ordered by telephone—would be sent to pick it up. It would be in a plain suitcase. There would be plenty of other people around in the station, coming and going from the checkroom. Carrying suitcases exactly like it. The cops would have a job keeping track of one of them; they'd be almost sure to give themselves away if they tried. If they did, though, if they did follow that plainclothes messenger, they wouldn't catch Uncle Bud.

He knew a stumblebum, a wino with a criminal record. The guy would do anything for a few bucks, no questions asked, and the suitcase would be delivered to him at this flophouse he lived in. If nothing happened after about an hour, Uncle Bud would pick it up. If something did happen—if the cops grabbed the guy—well, it was just too bad for him. He'd be caught with the evidence. He'd talk, of course, but he couldn't prove anything. Uncle Bud would just say that the guy was lying, and that would be that.

No, Uncle Bud wasn't taking any chances on anything. Chances were for the other guy—me. He'd already let me take them all, and now he was going to take all the money.

He was there in my mind, smiling and explaining—and laughing at me. All set to take the money—*my money* and laughing about it. Laughing, laughing, laughing, and there had to be some way, I had to find some way to stop him somehow . . .

I went to sleep.

. . . It was late when I woke up. Around noon. I saw what time it was, and I jumped out of bed fast. Kind of frightened, feeling that something was wrong, that some-one must have pulled something on me all those hours I'd been asleep.

I looked under the magazine, and that was all right. The gun was right where I had left it. The door was all right, too, still closed tight like I'd left it with a chair hooked under the knob. I looked out the window, pulling on my pants.

The car hadn't been moved. It stood in exactly the same spot as it had last night. There was no one coming up the lane, and everything seemed the way it should be. No! Someone *was* coming.

Fay. She was coming out of the house, carrying a coffee tray. She was coming toward the garage, and she was dressed as she had been a few mornings ago—the day that Doc Goldman had called her and everything had started going to pieces.

Bare legs, bare shoulders, ivory-colored in the sunlight. Tan shorts, curved to the curves of her thighs; and the thin white blouse, drawn tight, straining softly with the flesh beneath it.

She saw me staring at her, and smiled. She paused beneath the window, looked up smiling. And if last night's whiskey had left any marks on her, I sure didn't notice. She looked just as fresh and beautiful as she had that other morning.

Her eyes were as sparkling and crystal clear as I remembered. Her hair had that same soft, brushed-shiny look, and her face was the same rose-and-white softness.

Everything was the same. It was like that other morning all over again; as though it was still that morning and everything since then had been a bad dream.

"Well?" She smiled up at me. "Like to have some?"

I nodded. Or shook my head. Or something. I managed to mumble that I did.

"Some coffee, I mean?" she said.

And then she laughed and started toward the steps.

17

I let her into the room, and set the tray down for her. I acted, tried to act, just like she did, friendly and joking and laughing. But I figured that there must be something wrong, that she just about had to be working up to some kind of trick. So I gave her a good chance—a chance that *looked* good—to spring it.

I excused myself and went into the bathroom. I turned on the water in the sink, and then I tiptoed back to the door on my bare feet and peered out through a crack.

Fay was still in her chair, several feet away from the bed. I watched for a couple of minutes, thinking—and hoping that she wouldn't—thinking that she'd look under the pillow for the gun; that she'd do some more fast looking when she didn't find it there. Getting the gun was just about the only thing she could be up to. And if she didn't try for it, then what was she up to?

She didn't. She stayed there in the chair, one bare leg crossed over the other; kind of humming to herself.

I washed and went back into the room. She poured two cups of coffee, and handed me one. The boy seemed to be feeling fine, she said. Very lively. He'd eaten two poached eggs and a glass of milk.

"He wanted to get up, but I wouldn't let him. I thought he should stay in bed, don't you?"

I nodded. And I thought that maybe he was the reason for this. With him feeling pretty good, why she wasn't so worried anymore; she was feeling pretty good herself.

I frowned, not realizing that I did. Just thinking so hard, you know. Thinking and hoping that things might really be like they looked. She frowned, too, a sort of shamed expression crossing her face, shamed and kind of doubtful. And then she smiled again.

"Yes, Collie? Yes, my pugilist Apollo?"

"Well—" I hesitated. "Well, I was just wondering—"

"And I. And I don't seem to be able to explain. I suppose—" She paused and shrugged. "I suppose I said it all in the beginning. I'm just a crazy, mixed-up neurotic—anyone who drinks as I do, for as long as I have, is bound to be pretty shaky in the cerebrum. He—she, I should say—was an unstable character to begin with, and the booze makes her a lot worse than she was. It takes very little to throw her out of kilter. Very little. And what I've taken in these past few days has been somewhat more than a little. So—"

She put her coffee cup down. She glanced at me, took my cup, and put it down with hers.

"So?" she said. "So Collie?"

I nodded that I understood. And I thought I did, pretty well. Those institutions have a lot of alcoholic inmates. No one can be nicer or smarter than they are when they've leveled off. And no one can be as downright onery and crazy when they're in a bad way.

"Let's see." She tilted her head to one side. "Didn't we have a date a few mornings ago? Did we or not, Collie, do you remember?"

"Fay, I—I—"

"Words fail you, huh?" She laughed softly. "Well, let's

hope it isn't symptomatic of any physical weakness. Now, if you'll just step into the bathroom . . ."

"The—the bathroom?" I stammered.

"That small room you were in a moment ago. The one with the concave furniture."

I got up and went into the bathroom. I heard her draw the shade, and I started to jerk the door open. Then I saw what she was doing, and I stayed where I was until she called to me.

Her shoes were on the floor beside a chair. Her blouse was on the chair, and so were the shorts. She was lying on the bed, her black hair spread out on the pillow.

She held out her arms to me.

. . . There are some things you can't fake, you can't pretend about, and that's one of them. A person wants you that way, or she doesn't, and you always know which. And I knew which it was with her. The want was there. There wasn't a second of pretense in that long hour we were together. So even if Fay had a reason—and, of course, she did—for allowing the want to take over, there wasn't any faking afterwards. That was genuine, if nothing else was.

Now, she was gone. She'd dressed and gone over to the house to see how the boy was. And I stayed there on the bed. Because she was coming back in a few minutes. She was just going to look in on the boy, she wanted to check to see if Uncle Bud had been calling, and then she'd be back. She'd be back there with me, any minute now. We'd be together again—Fay and I would be together. And this time, we'd talk things out.

I'd find out how she really felt about the boy. Whether she didn't really feel like I did, that if we could get him back to his family safe and sound nothing else would matter much. We wouldn't have to give ourselves up, although there was a good chance that the cops would catch up with us in time. We could just leave the boy here, say—or leave him some place where he'd be comfortable and safe. Then, we could beat it, and send back word where to find him. That would fix Uncle Bud, keeping him from getting money. If we did get caught, finally, things would sure go a lot easier on us. We'd done something pretty bad, but if we did our best to straighten it out . . .

Of course, it wouldn't be our best that way. What we ought to do was call the cops right now; give up without waiting to be caught. But I didn't think that I could go that far, and I was positive that she couldn't. A person that drinks a lot is always frightened. They may act just the opposite—tough and hard, like they don't give a damn for anything. But inside they're scared. They have too much imagination. Everything is magnified in their minds, made a hundred times worse than it actually is. And a thing like this, facing a kidnaping rap, was plenty scary without any magnifying.

So we'd just do the best we were capable of. If she felt like I did, if that was what she wanted. Like I'd told her, the boy was sure to be all right for a day. We could leave him here, or someplace else; then, beat it and tip off the cops where he was. We didn't have much money—I didn't have any and she couldn't have a great deal. But we'd get by some way, and the boy would be all right. Right now nothing else seemed to matter much.

I lighted a cigarette and lay down again. Wondering just how I could work around to the subject, hoping that she would bring it up first. Wishing I wasn't still suspicious of her, and that she wasn't of me. Because, of course, she was and I was. There hadn't been much between us but suspicion and distrust these last few days. It couldn't all be wiped away in an hour.

Even right now, I guessed, if she should make the proposition to me—suggest doing what I wanted to do—I'd be a little leery of it. I'd think she was just trying to test me out, find out what I was thinking so that she could make sure I didn't go through with it. And if I felt that uneasy about her, she was bound to feel the same way about me, only a hell of a lot more so.

I was a mental case. I was an escapee from an insane asylum, a psycho with a gun, an ex-pug who could do plenty without a gun if he took a notion. I was that—and she was the other, a kind of mental case herself. Unstable, always afraid inside. Trying to drown the fear in booze and always having it float to the top stronger than ever.

It would be hard for her to talk straight with me. Probably

it would be just about impossible. She'd done just about all she could, I guess, toward breaking the ice. The rest would be up to me, and how I was going to go about it I didn't know. But I figured that it ought to be a lot easier after what had happened.

She must think a lot of me or she wouldn't have done it. Fay had to care, didn't she? Or did she?

She hadn't been faking, but maybe that didn't mean that she really cared. She'd been batting around on her own a long time. Drinking so much she didn't know what she was doing, or not giving a damn if she did know. Hanging out in joints like Bert's; getting on close terms with guys like Bert and Uncle Bud. A woman like that . . .

But Fay wasn't a woman like *that*. Like it seemed she might be. She wasn't cheap, shoddy, whatever else she was. She wasn't that, even if this was some kind of a trick. And I sure hoped that it wasn't for her sake, and mine. Because a guy like me, you sure never want to try to trick him.

For one thing, you probably won't get away with it. He's watching for it, he's thought of every angle you might try to play. You make just one little move toward one of them, and he's in there ahead of you. Moving in fast on you. He won't take any explanations. If you're smart, you won't try to give him any. You tricked him—tried to take advantage of him. That's all he sees. And about all you can do from then on is to keep out of his way. If you can. If he'll let you. For he'll never completely trust you again. He'll be watching you closer than ever, and if you take one little step in the wrong direction—or even look like you are—you'll never take another one.

I'd already had a fast one or two pulled on me. I was already damned watchful. I didn't want to be—I wanted to be able to trust Fay—but I just couldn't help it. So I sure hoped this wasn't some kind of a trick.

I heard the kitchen door slam. I pulled the shade back and glanced out the window. She was coming across the yard. She had a dress on, and she was walking pretty fast; and yet she seemed to be sort of dragging her feet, hanging back. As though she was working against herself, forcing herself forward.

I felt the tension coming back. I sat up and began putting on my clothes, shoving the gun into my hip pocket. I heard her coming up the stairs. I reached for my shoes, and started putting them on as she opened the door.

She came in. She looked at me, her face stiff, her eyes nervous and frightened. I straightened up and stared at her.

"What's up?"

"Collie, I—I—" She hesitated, took a deep breath. "I just talked with Uncle Bud, Collie."

"Yeah?"

"I—he thinks we'd better come over there right away! I c-called him, and that's what he said, Collie."

I nodded. I finished tying my shoelaces, and stood up. She backed away a step.

"Go on. Why does Uncle Bud think we'd better come over there right away? Don't you think maybe I'd better know?"

Her eyes wavered. Her face twitched as she tried to smile back at me. And then I guess she saw that I wasn't smiling, that it just looked like a smile. She backed away another step.

"You'd better watch out," I said. "You'll be out the door in a minute. You might fall over the banister and break your neck."

Fay looked over her shoulder quickly. She looked back at me, lips trembling, her face getting whiter than ever. I wondered how she'd ever gotten up the nerve to try this—even to get this far with the trick she was pulling. And knowing how frightened she was, I guess I should have liked and admired her for trying. But I didn't. What I felt toward her was anything but liking and admiration.

"Go on. You're not afraid to tell me, are you, Fay? After all, two people as close as us; sweethearts, I guess you'd call us—they shouldn't be afraid of each other."

A touch of red came into her face. She took another deep breath, hesitated, and then at last she got it out.

"The boy, C-Collie. He's run away!"

I nodded and gave her a smile—a smile that wasn't one. I said that, well, there wasn't anything to get too excited about. The shape the boy was in, he couldn't have gone very far. He was probably over in the house, hiding somewhere.

"N-no!" Fay shook her head. "I looked before I called Uncle Bud."

"Well, let me look. We'll look together. Stay nice and close together, you know, so that if one of us sees something he can point it out to the other."

"B-but—"

"That's what we'll do. And we'll do it right now."

I took her by the arm, pushed her through the door. We went down the steps, across the yard, and into the house. We started going through the rooms, with me talking and kind of joking, and Fay stammering and answering me in almost a whisper.

"Well, his clothes are gone. It sure looks like he dressed himself and ran off."

"Collie. We've got to—"

"Yes, sir. That's just the way it looks. And it looks like he probably did it when you were over there with me. When we were both pretty busy, with the shades pulled, and we weren't paying much attention to anything for about an hour. That's when it happened—it looks like."

I grinned at her. I let go of her arm suddenly, let go with a jerk that jerked her shoulder.

"We've got to leave, Collie! He's had plenty of time to get to the highway."

"He wouldn't get that far. I'm sure of it, and so is Uncle Bud. Otherwise, he wouldn't be coming anywhere near here."

"B-but—"

"Uncle Bud thinks the same thing that I do, that he's passed out somewhere right around here. He's got to that place, some nice secluded spot where no one can see him, and that's as far as he'll go. That's what Uncle Bud thinks—and I got a hunch it's what you think."

"No! Aaah, no, Collie! I wouldn't—"

"I told you. I told you that boy had to stay alive, and I told you why he had to stay alive. Now, where is he? Where did you leave him?"

"I—I—" She shook her head. "Is that what you think of me? D-do you really think I'd do that to him."

And for a moment I wavered. For a moment, I could almost see why she'd done it—and why she'd done it in this way. Fay was afraid. She wasn't sure of what I wanted to do, so she'd tried to take the decision out of my hands. She'd hidden the boy, left him where he'd be safe until she could get word to the cops. Then, she'd told me he'd run away, so that we'd have to run. It was the only thing she could do, as she looked at it. It was practically the same thing that I'd been thinking about doing.

So . . . so I had it all figured out, almost. We were on the same side of the fence. We both wanted the boy to get back to his parents. That's the way I figured, the way I thought it was. But with a thing like this—a guy like me—figuring and thinking weren't enough. I needed Fay to tell me—just to come right out with the truth without any tricks or hedging around. It was all she'd've had to do . . . and she didn't do it.

She was too frightened, too anxious. And when a person's that way, they almost always do the wrong thing. And what she did was the worst thing she could possibly have done.

She'd just hit me with one trick. Now, while I was still rocking from it, fighting to hang onto myself because I thought so much of her—now, she hit me with another one.

"Collie . . ." She forced herself to smile. "Let's be nice, hmm? Let's—l-let's lie down a while, get all nice and calm so we can talk a-and . . ."

Fay came toward me, holding onto the smile; forcing herself every inch of the way. Her hand went up to the shoulder of her dress, tugged at it shakily, and slowly slid it down. She hesitated than, pleading mutely with her eyes. Blushing, shamed despite the fear. Then, she took hold of the other shoulder, and slid it down. And waited.

"S-shall we, Collie?" She was almost against me.

"What do you think?" I sneered and swung with my open hand.

Fay screamed and staggered backwards, doubled over and clutching at her breasts. She bumped into a chair, and screamed again. Then, she fell down on the sofa, sat there moaning, rocking back and forth.

"That was just a sample. Try something like that again, and I'll really clobber you!"

"*Y-you!*" Fay gasped. "You—you—" The rocking stopped. She raised her head slowly, and looked up at me. "I want you to know, I want you to remember I warned you. I'm going to kill you for that!"

"Maybe. Maybe you will. But right now you're going to do something else. Fast and no maybe!"

She didn't argue about it. Fay pulled her dress back up and led the way down through the trees. We came to the culvert that ran under the lane. She nodded and stood back, and I got down and lifted him out.

I didn't know whether he was just unconscious from the exertion, or whether he'd been slugged. But there was a big bruise on the right side of his forehead. I looked down at it, at him, so little and so limp in my arms. And then I looked at her. And if I'd had my hands free just then—well, it was a good thing for her that I didn't have.

We went back to the house and I put the boy down on the sofa. Fay stood watching, kind of defiantly, as I sponged his face and forehead with cold water.

He came to and whispered that he felt, "F-fine," when I asked him. I guessed that he wasn't really hurt, just weak and frightened by so many things he couldn't understand. Most of the "bruise" turned out to be dirt. He had a little knot there on his forehead, but the biggest part of it—what I'd thought was bruise—washed off.

"Well . . ." Fay sloshed whiskey into a glass; gulped it. "I guess I missed that time, didn't I? I didn't hit him hard enough."

"What happened? Did you fall down with him?"

"Did I?" She reached for the bottle again. "You've got all the answers. You tell me whether I did or not."

"I guess you probably did."

"You do, huh? You'd actually give me a break? Well, shove it, bright boy! I hit him, get me? I slugged him as hard as I could with a big rock. And if I'd had more time

I'd've beat his brains out!"

I told her to quiet down; she'd disturb the boy. Fay yelled that she didn't give a damn if she did disturb him.

"Why the hell should I? Didn't I try to kill him? Well, didn't I, you rotten, mean, hateful, son-of-a-bitch? Sure, I did! That's the kind of a dame I am! I meant to kill him! I tried to! *I did, I did, I did . . .*"

And I knew that she hadn't—I knew it in my heart—but still it was easy to believe that she had. Fay looked twenty years older, haggard and vicious, her eyes glaring crazily. She was all crazy meanness and viciousness, drained dry of everything else. And it was easy to believe she'd do anything.

I told her to shut up. She yelled all the louder, backing away as I moved toward her.

She'd never said anything dirty before—sharp and ornery, maybe, but never dirty. But now she cut loose; and the names she called me, the things she said. Well, I've heard some rough talk but never anything as bad as that. Some of the words, but never all at one time. No one had ever called me one of them without losing some teeth.

The red haze gathered in front of me. I had to get rid of it, let off steam some way, because if I didn't I'd kill her. So I started yelling myself. I shouted back at her, cursing, calling her names. I yelled and she yelled, and how long it went on I don't know. Everything was a screaming red haze, yells and filth and redness, and how long it lasted I don't know.

But it was long enough.

Long enough for him to stop his car in the drive. To come up the walk and onto the back porch.

Whether he knocked I don't know—we wouldn't have known with the noise we were making. Probably he did knock, then just walked right on in like doctors do.

We heard the screen door slam, and that brought us up short. The room went completely silent. But by then, he was right on top of us. He'd heard it all. And, of course, he'd seen the boy.

He sauntered forward, casually; winked at me and smiled at Fay. "Mrs. Anderson, isn't it? I'm Doctor

Goldman."

"H-how—" Her mouth twisted. "How do you do, doctor?"

"I just dropped in for a moment. I'm due at the office now, but I happened to be out this way and . . ." His voice trailed off, and he nodded toward the boy. "Your son? Collie didn't tell me you had any children."

"It's her nephew," I said. "He's just visiting here for a couple of days."

"I see. Fine looking boy. A little under the weather, is he?"

He strolled over to the sofa and sat down. Still acting casual. Acting as though he hadn't heard the racket we were making, as though he didn't know exactly who the boy was.

"Not feeling too well, eh, sonny? Never mind. You don't need to talk. Let's see if I don't have something to . . ." He opened his medicine kit, snapped it shut again. "No, I guess not. I remember I was looking for some this morning before I left the office."

He bent over the boy a minute or two longer. Afraid to look around, I guess. Nerving himself for what he was going to do. Then he stood up carelessly and picked up the kit.

"He could do with a B-1 shot," he said. "You might mention it to his mother. I'd give him one, but I haven't any with me."

"A-all right." Fay shot a glance at me. "Thank you, doctor."

"Don't mention it. Just sorry I couldn't do something for him."

He smiled and nodded to us—or, to be more exact, to the space between us. Then, he moved toward the doorway, looking at the floor just ahead of him, making a big business out of buttoning his coat.

He paused, looking down. He went a couple of steps further, and came to another stop. I watched him silently, then crossed in front of him.

Outside; the wind rustled the dead grass, and the curtains swirled away from the windows. They fell back softly, flattening against the screens. And in the kitchen the clock ticked off the seconds.

Fay's breath went out in a sigh. Doc looked up. His eyes wavered at first, then they steadied and held mine.

"How did it happen Collie? How could you have done it?"

I shook my head. I didn't really know how it had happened. It seemed simple enough, taken step by step, but I couldn't explain now. And explaining wouldn't change anything.

"Get out of the way," he ordered. "Do you hear me, Collie? Stand out of the doorway at once!"

I shook my head again. Waiting for him to make the first move. Wishing he'd get it over with, so that I could do what I had to.

"You don't know what you're doing, Collie. I'm sure Mrs. Anderson can't realize what she's doing. Someone has duped you into this; they're using you for their own criminal purposes."

"It doesn't make any difference, Doc. You're not going anywhere. We're leaving and you're going to stay."

"No, Collie! You can't—" He bit his lip, looked at Fay. "Can't I appeal to you, Mrs. Anderson? Can't you understand, make him understand?"

"Fay," I said, "we're leaving. Get together anything you want to take and go on out to the car."

I stared into his eyes, waiting and watching. Fay circled around behind him and went into her bedroom.

There was another gust of wind. The grass rustled again and the curtains swirled. And in the kitchen the clock ticked off the seconds.

"Well," Doc said. "Well." He shrugged. "I suppose, if that's the way it has to be . . ."

He turned. Then, he whirled suddenly, hurled the medicine kit and dived for the door. I ducked and swung all in one motion. I pulled the punch, but it landed right on the button.

Doc's head snapped back. His knees buckled, and I had to catch him to keep him from falling. I picked him up and carried him into the bedroom.

. . . His answering service knew that he'd come here.

They phoned, just as I finished binding and gagging him with his own adhesive tape. I told them he wouldn't get back to the office today. He was tied up on an emergency, and they were to check here again in the morning.

Fay was already waiting in the car. I put the boy down on the floor in the rear, got in with him, and we drove off fast. Down the lane and into the highway. Headed for Uncle Bud's place.

Rushing toward the end.

Uncle Bud kept on the move, switching from one place to another. But I guess that every place he lived would always be just about like the others. It would have the same features.

It would be a dump because he was tight with his money; because he seldom stayed at home if he had any place else to go. It would be fairly close in, a place he could circulate from easily. It would be a place you'd probably never find by yourself, one he'd have to tell you how to find.

This one—the place we went to that day when everything began rushing toward the end—was in the city's old business district. Or on the edge of it, I should say. Fifty years ago it had been the main part of town, but then the railroad station had been moved and the highways built around the city instead of passing through it. That had put it on the downgrade, and now it was about as far down as it could go.

Flop houses. Two-bit hotels. Cheap bars and greasy-spoon restaurants. That was about all you saw there now, and you didn't see any of them after the first few blocks. After that there were just empty buildings, or vacant lots where the buildings had been torn down, until you came to a bridge, a kind of a viaduct. It crossed the abandoned railroad right-of-way and opened into the abandoned highway. Right at the foot of it was an old garage building—well-built and still in pretty good shape—with living quarters on the second floor. And that was where

Uncle Bud lived.

I drove the car into the garage part. Uncle Bud was waiting for us, and he led the way upstairs. He wasn't at all upset about what had happened. It didn't change the picture at all, he said. Not that much, Kid; no, sir, not even that much. Everything was working out fine and dandy, and we'd all be wearing diamonds in another day or two.

Fay went into the bedroom with the boy. Uncle Bud nudged me, whispered that I didn't want to be too hard on the little lady. She was just jumpy, like little ladies got sometimes, and it was up to me and him to keep our heads, now, wasn't it?

"I'm going to. That's just what I'm going to do, Uncle Bud."

"Atta boy! You're my kind of people, Kid. Now, you just sit tight here, and I'll get you fixed up right."

I looked him over as he left. I gave him another good once-over when he came back and started piling groceries, beer, and whiskey on the table. And I saw that he wasn't packing a gun. Things were working out real nice for him, he thought, and there was nothing he needed a gun for.

"Well, Kid." He motioned toward the table. "See anything I overlooked? Anything you think of, just name it."

"You've got plenty. We're not going to need all that."

"Well, you can't never tell now. I want you and Fay to be comfortable, and you may have to hole up here quite a while."

I grinned to myself. I said I was sure we'd have plenty of everything.

"Yeah?" He gave me a sharp look. "But they'll find that doctor in the morning, won't they? You won't be able to do no chasing around after that."

"That's right," I said.

"Well, uh, well," he said hastily, "what I meant was, you might want something and I wouldn't be around to get it for you."

"Sure. But we'll have plenty. You don't have to worry about that at all."

He hesitated, started to say something else. Then, he gave up on it—chalked it up, I guess, to some more of my screwy talk—and uncorked a bottle of whiskey. We poured drinks. He went on with the gabbing, talking about how fine everything was. And I nodded and grinned and told him he was sure right.

The fun was going to be over pretty soon. Pretty soon, now, I was going to set him back on his heels. So I let him enjoy himself while he could.

Fay came out of the bedroom and fixed the boy an egg and some milk. I watched from the doorway as she tried to feed it to him, and it was just no go. He just didn't have the strength or the stomach for it.

She brought the plate and the glass back into the kitchen. Uncle Bud pulled his everything-is-fine line on her, and she stood and looked at him until he was all through. Until the words kind of died in his throat. Then, she filled a glass with whiskey and sat down in a corner with it.

Evening came on. Uncle Bud got busy with the food, made a plate of lunch-meat sandwiches and opened up some potato salad and a few cans of stuff.

I ate a pretty good meal. Fay took a sandwich and more whiskey. Uncle Bud didn't eat anything.

"I'll just grab me a bite later," he said, taking a big swallow of his drink. "I ain't real hungry now, so I'll just get something when I go into town."

I didn't say anything. He took another drink, fidgeting a little.

"I still got to keep right on top of this deal, y'know, Kid. This is the most important time. We're due to pull down the money in less than twenty-four hours. And if the cops got any fast ones cooking—they might try to pull something right at the last minute, you know—why, it's up to me to find out about it."

I waited, still keeping silent. Looking at him, and saying nothing. He filled up his glass again.

"Yeah," he mumbled. "Yes, sir, I sure got to keep a close eye on everything from now until the wind-up. You, uh, I guess you and Fay can get along here all right by yourselves, huh?"

I smiled at him. Just smiled. He glanced nervously at Fay, and she gave him a dead-eyed stare.

"I guess it all works out pretty good. We can't very well all of us stay here, so it's just as well that I'll be away. I, uh—" Uncle

Bud paused, fumbling with the buttons of his coat. "You're sure you don't need anything now? You'll be all right until tomorrow night? Well, I'll just run along then."

And I spoke at last. I told him to stay right where he was for a moment, and Fay and I and the boy would go with him.

He laughed. He put on his hat and started to get up. And then it registered on him, what I'd said, and he sank back down in his chair.

"G-go with me?" he stammered. "W-what—what for?"

"For the same reason you're going," I said. "To get the money."

His mouth dropped open. A guilty, red flush spread over his face. "K-Kid, I, I—it ain't the right time yet. You know it ain't, Kid! It's not supposed to be until tomorrow night!"

"Yeah? How do I know that?"

"Why—why, because! It's what we planned right from the beginning! I gave the family seventy-two hours."

"Seventy-two hours from when? From the time I took the boy? From the time the ransom note was mailed? From the time the family got it, or the night of the day they got it or when?"

"Well, it—it was—"

"Forget it. It doesn't mean anything. It doesn't change anything. Maybe you didn't plan on running out on us in the beginning, but you'd never pass up a setup like the one you've got now. Fay and me tied down here—the cops looking for us after tomorrow morning. You on the loose." I shook my head, nodded to Fay. "Get the boy ready. We're leaving."

She got up and went into the bedroom. Not saying a word. Ignoring him when he told her to wait, to talk the Kid out of this crazy notion. Fay shut the door. He stared at it helplessly.

"All right, Kid. The money ain't there, but if you won't take my word for it, I'll prove it to you. It's all wrong, sending the messenger now—showing our hand in advance—but if that's the way you got to have it—"

"It's not the way," I said. "We're going to pick the money up ourselves."

That one really threw him. Uncle Bud looked like he was about to faint.

"*No!*" he said. "No, you can't mean it, Kid. Take that boy into the railroad station? W-why, hell, we probably wouldn't much more'n get him out of the car before he was spotted."

"All right. We'll leave him in the car then. Just you and I and Fay will go in."

"Leave him? Damn it, that's even worse! He might start stirring around. Someone might look in and see him."

"That's right." I nodded. "And no one's going to do anything to him to make sure that he doesn't stir around."

"Well, then? You can see yourself that your idea won't work, Kid."

"Fay doesn't trust me. I don't trust her. And we don't trust you. But I can fix that part—you. We'll park near the station, where I can see you go in and come out. If you aren't back in fifteen minutes, I'll tip the cops off to you."

"But—Kid! Kid." Uncle Bud mopped his face. "That—it just ain't right! Suppose the money really isn't there?"

"It is. We both know it is. So get it. Get it by yourself, or Fay and I will go with you and get it."

"But you can't! You can't leave the boy in the car like that."

"So that brings us right back where we started from, doesn't it? You get it, and don't take more than fifteen minutes to do it."

"B-but—"

His mouth worked helplessly. He looked down at the floor, shaking his head, wagging it back and forth, until I thought it was going to fall off. And, then, at last he looked up again, there was a kind of greenish cast to his face, but a red flush was spreading beneath it. Uncle Bud was sick—really sick, he was scared so bad. But along with it he was ashamed.

"Kid, I guess I got to tell you something. This deal—I—there wasn't much risk the way I had it figured. With the messenger picking up the money, you know, and that wino to take the fall if there was one. I—well, I didn't have to know if there was a police stake-out at the pay-off place. I mean, if there was it wouldn't catch me. I wouldn't lose nothing but the dough. I—I—" He licked his lips.

"Go on."

"Well, uh, about the money. About maybe it's being marked or the serials registered. There wasn't any risk there either, the way I figured. Hell, all those small bills— the biggest ones twenties—they just couldn't trace 'em. There's too many in circulation, and by the time they traced 'em back to a guy, why—well, I didn't believe they could. I didn't think the family would play around to begin with, they'd be so anxious about the boy. And if they or the cops did try anything funny, it wouldn't get them anywhere. So . . . so." He paused, glanced at me pleadingly. "You see what I mean, Kid? You see what I'm driving at?"

I nodded. I saw it, and I felt sorry for him. But not as sorry as he wanted me to feel, not after what he'd done to me. Except for him, I wouldn't be in this spot. I wouldn't have hurt Doc, the only man who'd ever done anything for me. And the little boy wouldn't be dying. And Fay and I— things might have been a lot different between us. You couldn't judge by the way things were now. We'd both been pretty mixed up, easy to swing one way or another, and we might have swung the right way instead of this one. We might have. It could have worked out that way.

If Uncle Bud had left us alone.

"I've been lying to you, Kid. I don't have no pipelines into the department. Most, of the guys I know, they don't even speak to me any more. They see me comin' they turn the other way. I guess I can't blame them much, but anyway that's the way it is. I don't know what they're doing or what they've done. I figured I could get by safe enough without knowing. If there was any kind of jam, it would be someone else that got stuck, and—and naturally, I didn't want no one else to get into trouble."

"Let it go at that. You don't know anything. You're not sure that the guy who goes for the money won't be walking into a police trap."

"That's right, Kid."

"Well, you'll know pretty soon," I said. "You're going to

find out awfully fast."

. . . We sat there for another half-hour or so, and he was talking every minute of it. Begging, pleading with me, actually crying a little toward the last. The words poured out of his mouth, and they didn't mean a thing to me. I didn't even hear them. They were just a noise, just a lot of noises coming from a sickish-white face. I didn't mind them particularly. I didn't care whether Uncle Bud made them or whether he didn't. Other people had never meant anything to him. What they said meant nothing to him. And now it was his turn. Now, he was meaningless, and what he said was meaningless.

I was all those other people, all the people in the world, and I couldn't see him and I couldn't hear him.

He stopped talking, at last. He'd talked himself kind of hoarse. I finished my drink, and set the glass on the table.

"Anything else? If-you're all through, we'll shove off."

"S-shove off? But, Kid, I just—" .

"All right. There's no hurry. You talk as long as you want to, and then we'll leave."

His eyes watered. His lips trembled, and he managed to get his mouth open, but no words came out. I grinned at him. I asked him again if there was anything he wanted to say.

Uncle Bud looked at me dully, hesitated, and made one last try. "I know quite a few people around that station, Kid. Guys that ain't got much use for me. If one of 'em should get in touch with Bert—"

"Go on. Make it nice and scary."

"It could happen, Kid! He always comes into town for dinner, and if he had the word spread around to look out for me— And you know he has! You know he's been tipped off!"

"Uh-uh. I don't know it, and neither do you."

"Don't make me do it, Kid!" His eyes filled with tears again. "Please don't make me do it. If one of those guys should call Bert, he could be there in five minutes."

"Only five minutes?" I grinned. "You don't think he could make it in three?"

"I'm beggin' you, Kid! I got a bad feeling about this. If the cops don't get me, why—"

"Shut up! Get up and start moving. I'm sick of looking at you."

I rode in the back with the boy. Fay drove, and Uncle Bud sat in the front with her. There wasn't a half-dozen words passed between us on the way into town. About three blocks from the railroad station, I had Fay stop the car and Uncle Bud got out.

It was about seven-thirty, the quiet part of the evening. The day rush was over, and it was too early for the dinner and theatre crowds.

Uncle Bud trudged down the street, practically by himself. He turned around near the end of the block and looked back at us. He crossed the intersection and looked back again. He hesitated, sort of teetering—too scared to go ahead, knowing it was go ahead or else. Then he went on, walking fairly fast. Anxious, I guess, to get the job and the suspense over with.

I got behind the wheel and made the boy lie on the floor in back. Then I followed Uncle Bud down the street, letting the car creep along, letting him stay well ahead of me.

The railroad station occupied a block on the other side of the street. I stopped in the middle of the block just below it and shut off the motor. I watched as Uncle Bud went up the broad marble steps and disappeared through the entrance.

I scooted down a little in the seat and peered up at the clock in the station tower. It was twenty minutes of. He had until five of eight to get back with the money. If he wasn't back by then . . .

I kind of hoped that he wouldn't be. Because I'd meant just what I'd said about calling the cops, and that would wind everything up just that much faster. And that was all I wanted now. Just to get it over with, to have the end come. Because it was bound to be bad; no good, no happiness, could come out of this now, so the quicker it was over the better.

I'd have ended it myself if I could have. But somehow I

couldn't, and I guess it wasn't so strange that I couldn't. There's something inside of every man that keeps him going long after he has any reason to. He's no good to life and life is no good to him, and he knows it will always be that way. But still he can't quit. Something keeps prodding him, whispering to him—making him hope in the face of hopelessness. Making him believe there's a reason to stay in there and pitch, and that if he fights long enough he'll stumble onto it.

It's that way with everyone, or almost everyone, I guess. It's hardly ever been any other way with me. For years, for as far back as I could remember, I'd kept going when going didn't seem to make any sense. And I had to keep on now. If any quitting was done, it had to be done for me.

Uncle Bud had been gone a little more than five minutes. It was five minutes, I mean, since he'd entered the station. I looked down from the clock to the tall doors of the building, and I saw a man hurry through one of them and pause at the top of the steps. He had something in his hand—a flashlight. He flashed it three times, and the light was red.

It didn't mean anything to me for a minute. I just thought, still, there's a guy with a red flashlight, so what about it? Then, Fay sat up with a gasp, turned toward me, her face blurred white in the semi-darkness. "Collie! L-look!" she said and pointed. But I was already looking, for the street had suddenly come to life.

A police car had pulled into each side of the intersection ahead of us. Two other cars had stopped at the next intersection, shutting off the side streets. And in the block beyond, a car was out in the middle of the intersection, and a cop was directing traffic off of the street.

"Collie!" Fay whispered. "Collie! W-what are they doing?"

"It's a stake-out. They tagged him as soon as he got the money, but they're afraid to take him in a crowd. I guess that's the reason."

"Well do somethin'! L-let's get out of here! Aah, Collie, I—I—"

I kind of frowned, jerked my arm away from her hand. This was what I wanted, you see, the end. And it seemed like she should want it, too; that she should damned well get it, regardless of what she wanted. Because Fay wasn't fit to live, because she'd be better off dead or locked up for life. And I started to tell her that. And then—

When a man stops caring what happens, all the strain is lifted from him. Suspicion and worry and fear—all the things that twist his thinking out of focus—are brushed aside. And he can see people as they are, at last. Exactly as they are—as I saw Fay then.

Weak and frightened. Self-pitying, maybe. But good, too. Basically as good as a woman could be, and hating herself for not being better. She'd planned to call the cops, telling them the boy was in the culvert, after we'd made our escape. I *knew* that now. I knew that if it came to a show-down, she'd protect him with her life. I *knew* it, and suddenly I wanted Fay to live.

Suddenly, it made sense for Fay to live; it was the only way my having lived would make any sense. It was why I had lived, it seemed like. It was why I had been made like I was. To show her something, to prove something—to do something for her that she could not do for herself. And, then, to protect her so that she could go on. So that she would have the reason for living that I'd never had.

I turned on the switch key. Then, I glanced over my shoulder, hesitated, and turned it off again. Because it was too late, of course. The whole area had been blocked off at the same time. The street behind us was blocked, and a motorcycle cop was bearing right down on us.

I barely had time to check that the boy was down flat, when he drew up at the side of the car, bracing his feet on the pavement. I looked out the window, smiling at him, and he turned the flashlight into my face. He held it on me for a moment, then switched it over to Fay, then brought it back to me again.

"Something wrong?" I said, hoping he wouldn't see the boy on the floor in back. "Aren't we supposed to park here, officer?"

He grunted as he held the light on my face.

"What's all the excitement about?" I said. "Why all the police cars? My wife and I were just sitting here and—"

"Why?" He snapped off the light. "What business you got here? Who you waitin' for?"

He was an older man, maybe fifty. He was kind of heavy-set, like motor cops get, and he had a fat, hard-looking face.

"We're waiting for a friend of mine, Jack Billingsley. He's coming in from the East about eight-thirty, coming in on the train, and we were waiting for him."

"What's your name? This your car? Let's see the papers on it," he said all in one breath.

I gave him my right name, William Collins. "This is our car, all right, but we left the house in kind of a hurry tonight and I'm not sure that—" I glanced at Fay. "I guess you've got the papers with you, haven't you, honey? In your purse, maybe?"

She got her purse open, fumbled it open. She began pawing through it, moving the stuff it was filled with this way and that. The cop scowled suspiciously and bent close to me.

"I've seen you some place before. What'd you say your name was?"

"Collins. We're waiting for a friend of mine, Jack Billingsley. He's due on the train soon."

"I've seen you. Ever been in any trouble? What do you do for a living? How about them papers, lady?"

"No, I haven't been in any trouble. You must have me mixed up with someone else. I'm retired now, but I used to—"

"I ain't got you mixed up. I've seen you. Let's see your driver's license."

He glanced over into the back of the car. I thought of the boy and I reached for the gun in my pocket, but he jerked his eyes back to me. Then he turned the flashlight into my face again.

And suddenly he grabbed me by the arm.

"Hold it!" The light filled my eyes, blinding me. "What'd you say your name was?"

"Collins."

"Yeah. Yeah, why sure, it is!" He laughed and let go of my arm. "Kid Collins, why, sure. It was on the West Coast. I won twenty-five bucks on you."

He shook hands, leaned in and shook hands with Fay. "You say you're retired now, Kid? Livin' here in town, are you? Didn't mean to give you and your wife a bad time, but it's been so long ago and you being right here where all this is happening . . ."

"What's going on?" I said innocently. "Some kind of trouble?"

"You said it." He glanced over his shoulder. "Let's see. Don't believe you'd better try to pull out now, but maybe . . . Back it up a ways, Kid. Get back there around the middle of the block."

I started the car and put it in reverse. He backed up with me, kind of pushing himself along with his feet. And I had to watch where I was going, of course, and keep an eye on him, too. So that was why I missed what went on.

I didn't see Uncle Bud come out of the station. Uncle Bud with the suitcase, and Bert right on his heels. I didn't see him try to break and run from Bert. I was looking behind me until I heard the shot, and by the time I got turned around it was all just about over.

Uncle Bud was sprawled on the steps. Bert had grabbed up the suitcase and was heading back toward the station entrance. And he's got just about two steps when the cops inside cut loose on him—the detectives who had been waiting in there.

He screamed. I heard the one scream above the blast of their guns. Then, he toppled over backwards, still hanging onto the suitcase, went tumbling and rolling down the steps until his body struck the sidewalk.

"Well, that's it." The cop nodded to me. "Guess you'll have to pick up your friend a little later, Kid. This place is going to be pretty hot for a while."

"Yeah. It kind of looks like it would all right."

"Just make you a U-turn right here, and I'll signal for the boys to let you through."

I turned around in the street, and drove back to the intersection. He signaled, the cops let me through, and I kept on going.

I drove almost until dawn, just driving aimlessly, just riding—going on—until it was time to stop going. I didn't know when that time would be, but I figured it couldn't be very far off. And I knew I'd know it when it did come. Things would work out a certain way, so that I could stop living and Fay could go on. It would all work out in time, just a little more time, and meanwhile I had to keep going.

Finally, a little before daylight, I turned off the highway and into an old trail. It was so overgrown with weeds and grass you could hardly see it, and it faded off into a sort of jungle of underbrush. But I ploughed the car on through it. And after a few hundred yards, the ground sloped downwards to a creek. It was practically dried up, just a little trickle of water between two high banks, so I turned the car into it and stopped. I had to. With a trail that no one would ever spot and with this archway of trees overhead, it was just what I needed. Exactly the right place to wait while things were working out a certain way. And now that I'd gotten to it, the car had run out of gas.

Fay had brought a full quart of whiskey with her from Uncle Bud's place. She'd started slugging it down as soon as we'd got out of that police trap, and now she had passed out.

I corked the bottle and sat it down on the floor. I looked back at the boy. He was asleep. Really asleep and not just unconscious. I tucked the blanket around him a little better and went to sleep myself. It was safe enough with Fay passed out. She'd be that way for hours, and I'd be sleeping pretty lightly.

I waked up around noon when the boy started stirring. I got out quietly, lifted him out, and laid him down on the ground. I scooped up some water in a rusty can and gave him a drink. Then, I let him go to the toilet, washed his face and hands for him, and put him back in the car. There was nothing else I could do for him, and he wanted to get back in. Just that little exertion had worn him out.

I got back in the car myself. There was still a good pint of whiskey in the bottle, a little more than a pint I mean, and that would be more than enough for Fay. So I took one pretty good drink of it and corked the bottle back up again.

It was the middle of the afternoon before Fay waked up. She took a drink and left the car for a few minutes. When she returned she looked at the boy, tried to talk to him—to ask him how he was, and so on. And then she got back into the seat with me and picked up the bottle.

"Well? What do we do now, stupid?"

I shrugged. "How do I know. You tell me if you've got any ideas."

"Hell!" She shook her head dully. "Hell! What a mess! The whole damned country looking for us. No money and no car and a kid that's as good as dead, and—" Her voice broke, and she took another big drink. "What a mess! What a combination! Everything else, and a lunatic to boot."

"I'm not crazy. I'm just—"

"No, you're not! You're just mean and rotten and no good! I could feel sorry for you if you were really crazy, but— Aah, forget it. Turn on the radio."

I turned it on. We sat listening all through the afternoon, and it was all pretty much the same thing. A lot of words built around a few facts. Or, I should say, what they thought were facts.

Bert and Uncle Bud had died before they could talk. The playground matron "believed" that Bert was the kidnaper, and the cops "believed" that he and Uncle Bud were the principals in the crime. Fay and I were kind of small fry, supposedly. Just a couple of stooges.

Then a familiar voice came over the radio—Doc Goldman's.

Doc Goldman wasn't sure that Fay was actually in on the deal. It was possible, he thought, that she might have been acting under coercion. As for me, well, I wasn't completely responsible for what I did. I knew what I was doing, so I could be held legally responsible. But I *had* tried to save the boy's life—I'd risked discovery and capture to steal that insulin. And it was just possible that I'd been forced to take part in the crime along with Fay. I could have been, even though I'd slugged him and tied him up. That was a natural reaction for a guy like me who thought he was in danger. Any time I got in a tight spot, I'd just about have to turn violent.

It was a pretty thin theory, of course; about me being coerced. I mean. There were all kinds of holes in it that I couldn't fill, and I sure wasn't going to try. Still, it *sounded* hopeful, taken along with some of the facts. And what Doc and the cops thought about Fay sounded a hell of a lot better. All she needed now was something to kind of top off their theories. To sew them all up tight and leave her in the clear.

Doc talked quite a while—about us and to us. He kept urging us to come in, if we had the boy. *If.* We couldn't get away. We'd have to give up sooner or later. So if the boy was alive, if Bert or Uncle Bud hadn't killed him, if he was with us . . .

The car battery was going dead. Doc's voice grew fainter and fainter, and finally it faded out entirely. And now it was night again.

I heard Fay take a drink. I heard her as she took another one, a long one, and dropped the bottle out of the side of the car. She'd be feeling pretty steady by this time. Her nerve would be built up, and that hard, ugly streak would be cropping out. She'd be up to anything in this mood.

And they didn't know that we had the boy. That motorcycle cop had said that we didn't, and the cops who'd let us through the street block said the same thing. Maybe they really believed they'd looked in the car, or maybe they were just trying to get themselves out of a jam. But, anyway, no one knew the truth.

Fay struck a match to a cigarette. It glowed in the darkness, lighting up her face as she took a long deep puff. "Well, we know what we have to do. Let's get it over with."

I nodded. I said, yeah, we might as well.

"One thing, Collie . . ." She hesitated, some of the sharpness going out of her voice. "You've done some pretty inexcusable things, but I know you weren't responsible. You thought you had to protect the boy from me. Whatever I said, I'm sorry."

"Forget it, Fay. It's all my fault. I thought it was smart to keep the boy alive, but I guess it's just about the dumbest thing I ever did."

"Well, regardless of who was at fault, I— *What?*" Her head snapped around. "Why, C-Collie, what do mean by that?"

"You don't get it? You call me stupid, and you don't see what I mean?"

"N-no. No, I don't see!"

"Aw, you've got to! Bert's stuck with the actual kidnaping, isn't he? He and Uncle Bud could be blamed for practically everything that I did, couldn't they? And you—"

"Collie!" she said sharply. "What are you getting at?"

"—And you," I went on, "you've got it just about perfect. It looks a hundred per cent better for you than it does for me. You were a woman living alone. Bert and Uncle Bud threatened you, and you were scared to death of me so you went along with us."

"I asked you, Collie. I asked you what you were getting at."

"You really don't get it?" I laughed. "Well, I guess you probably wouldn't at that. You're sitting pretty already, and it won't hurt you if the kid talks. But it'll hurt me plenty. So—so there's your answer, all spelled out for you. He's not going to do any talking."

Fay stared at me, silent and motionless for a moment. Then, still staring at me, she raised her hand and let the cigarette butt drop out the window. Slowly she shook her head.

"You don't mean that. You can't mean it. Y-you—you've been through more than even a normal person could take, and you're excited and frightened. You don't mean it, do you, darling. I know my Collie, and I know he'll—"

I laughed, cutting her off. "I really had you fooled, didn't I? Well, I guess I should, all the practice I've had. I started in almost fifteen years ago—I was up for a murder rap, see, and it was the only thing I could think of. So I went into the act, and it got me out from under. And then I went into the Army, and it got me out of that. It looked like such a sweet deal that I started working the act full time."

"*What* act?" she said. "W-what are you saying?"

"The crazy stuff." I laughed again. "Hell, it's better than a pension. I could just roam around doing what I pleased—acting stupid, and cracking down when people fell for it. Then, whenever I got tired, I'd just turn in at some institution for a while. Those places are pretty swell, you know; just like a high class country club. A swell private room and anything you want to eat. Hell, you never tasted anything like it! And you ought to see how people knock themselves

out to wait on you. Why, I was in one place where they had
a nurse for each patient. Real pretty ones, to keep you
cheered up and feeling good . . ."

I made it as strong as I knew how. Laughing and kidding
about it. Rubbing it in on her hard. And at first Fay cut in a
time or two, and then she just sat and listened. And, gradually, I felt the change in her. I could feel the last bit of uncer-
tainty giving way to coldness and hatred and disgust.

"I don't know why people never get wise," I said. "You
do all sorts of things to give yourself away—to prove, you
know, that you're plenty good at looking out for yourself.
But somehow they never seem to catch on. They go right
on falling for the act and feeling sorry for you."

I snickered and lighted a cigarette. I held the match for a
moment, while I took the gun from my pocket and checked
the chamber. "Well, I guess I'll get it over with."

As I expected, she made a wild grab for the gun. I jerked
it back and thrust it forward suddenly. Fay screamed as she
had that time back at the house.

"I won't kill you. I'll just mark you up real good, like
you'd been through a struggle. I was trying to keep you
from killing the boy, see, and the gun went off accidentally."

"D-don't," she sobbed. "Do anything you want to me,
but don't kill him."

"Now, there's a good idea. It's better than just bumping
off the brat and leaving him here. After all, it was Uncle
Bud's gun and you knew him a long time before I did."

I turned in the seat and opened the door. I slid the gun
back onto my hip, but not into the pocket. I let it slip past
the pocket—as though I'd missed and didn't know it—and
down onto the seat. Then I got out, my back turned to her.

There was one shattering explosion, and I pitched forward against the creek bank.

Everything was silent for a moment. Then, I heard Fay
scramble out of the car and take the boy out. Stagger away
with him, her footsteps growing fainter and fainter . . . and
then vanishing entirely. And I stayed where I was, unable
to turn, my face pressed into the dirt. And that was the way
it should be, I guessed, right where it had always been.
And this—this, what had happened, was, as it had to be.
She'd had to hate me. Fay had to go on hating me, thinking

what she did about me, as long as she lived. And . . . and that . . . that was the way it would be, too.

But I wished she'd stayed a little while longer. Just a little, the minute or two more that I was going to stay. And if she'd wanted to talk mean or call me dirty names, it would have been all right, because it was just her way, you know. Fay just . . . if she'd just—

. . . *"You silly looking goof! You couldn't sell cyanide in a suicide colony!"*

"I'm just waiting for a friend. Maybe you know him—Jack Billingsley? Big real-estate family. We were driving to California, and . . ."

"California, huh? Well, New York here I come!"

"The car broke down and I went for help, and I guess that darned crazy Jack Billingsley . . ."

"Jerk! Stupid! Souphound! Bark for me. Roll over and do some tricks . . ."

. . . I grinned, because she didn't really mean a thing by it, you know. I barked, I guess it sounded like a bark maybe; and my body jerked, rolled a little. And then I stopped.

I just kind of stopped all over.

About the Author

James Meyers Thompson was born in Anadarko,
Oklahoma, in 1906. He began writing fiction at a very
young age, selling his first story to *True Detective*
when he was only fourteen. In all, Jim Thompson
wrote twenty-nine novels and two screenplays (for the
Stanley Kubrick films *The Killing* and *Paths of
Glory*). Films based on his novels include *Coup de
Torchon (Pop. 1280)*, *Serie Noire (A Hell of a
Woman)*, *The Getaway*, *The Killer Inside Me*, *The
Grifters*, and *After Dark, My Sweet*. A biography of
Jim Thompson will be published by Knopf.